CROISSANTS AND CORRUPTION

A MARGOT DURAND COZY MYSTERY

DANIELLE COLLINS

FAIRFIELD PUBLISHING

CONTENTS

Copyright   v

Message to Readers   1
Chapter 1   2
Chapter 2   13
Chapter 3   22
Chapter 4   32
Chapter 5   44
Chapter 6   59
Chapter 7   70
Chapter 8   79
Chapter 9   92
Chapter 10   100
Chapter 11   108
Chapter 12   118
Chapter 13   129
Chapter 14   140
Chapter 15   147
Thank You!   153
Recipes   157
Book Previews   165

Thank you so much for buying my book. I am excited to share my stories with you and hope that you are just as thrilled to read them.

If you would like to know about all my new releases and have the opportunity to get free books, make sure you sign up for our Cozy Mystery Newsletter.

FairfieldPublishing.com/cozy-newsletter

CHAPTER 1

*I*t was the beginning of a perfect late spring day in North Bank, Virginia, despite the fact that the sun hadn't yet come up. The crisp air coming off the Potomac invigorated Margot Durand as she picked up her pace down the street on the way to her bakery, *The Parisian Pâtisserie.* It sat at the river's edge waiting for lights and the scent of baking pastries to fill the space.

It was a typical early morning—a baker's morning—aside from the fact that, as Margot unlocked the front door and rushed to disarm the alarm, her phone vibrated in her pocket.

Who in the world is calling me at three in the morning?

Depositing her bag on the counter and flipping on the bright halogen lights, she dislodged her phone from her back pocket and jammed her finger against the screen before she lost the call.

"Hello?"

"Heya, sis."

"Renee?" Margot blinked in shock. Her sister lived in California and, with a little mental math, Margot realized it was midnight for her. "Why are you calling me so...late?"

"It's early there, right?"

Margot nodded then remembered her sister couldn't see her. "Yes. I've just made it to the bakery."

"I figured..." Her sister trailed off, but Margot caught the hint of warning in her voice.

"Rae, what is it?"

After a lengthy silence, Renee said one word. "Taylor."

"Oh no." Margot dropped into her desk chair, swiveling her knees under the counter and propping her chin on her palm. "What's she done this time?"

An image of her niece—long blonde hair and the perfect California tan that came from living in Laguna Niguel— filled her mind. She was what, nineteen now? And there was no end to the grief she had given Renee.

"She's all but failed out of her second semester at Coastline Community College and I'm at my wit's end to know what to do with her. She's running around with a bunch of beach bum surfers and I swear she thinks she'll be able to live like that for the rest of her life. She has no

3

idea what hard work means and…" Her sister took in a shuddering breath. "I think she could be into drugs."

"Oh, Renee…" Margot shook her head, sending up a prayer for her sister's daughter as much as for her sister. "What will you do?"

Another long pause. So long, in fact, that Margot began to wonder if her sister was still on the line.

Finally, she spoke again. "I need to ask a huge favor."

A feeling of dread sunk into the pit of Margot's stomach. It was the same feeling she got when trying out a new recipe and knowing for a fact that it wasn't going to turn out.

"What do you mean?"

"Can you *please* take Taylor for the summer?"

"Take…her? What do you mean?"

"I don't care that she's old enough to make her own decisions." Renee's voice steeled as she went on. "I want to send her to live with you for the summer. I want her to work for you. I think showing her how rewarding owning your own business can be will be a really great thing for her. It may even save her life, Marg."

Save her life.

The words echoed through Margot but the terror remained. "Are you crazy?"

Renee laughed. "I've been accused of worse."

"No, I mean, what makes you think she'll want to stay with me?"

"Because we're cutting her off if she doesn't go."

"Cutting her off?" Margot repeated the words, trying to make sense.

"We've been footing the bill for her little escapades, but no longer. We're giving her an ultimatum. She either goes to stay with you *and* work for you for the summer, or she's… out of the house." Her sister's voice broke on the last word.

"I'm so sorry, Rae. That's not something you want to say about your own daughter."

"No." Her sister let out a heavy sigh. "With Dillon working on that oil rig months at a time, I haven't had the strength —or the clout—to deal with this. Am I a bad mother, Marg? You know it was hard for me to step in like this…"

"Of course you're not a bad mother!" Margot was quick to reassure her sister. "You've done a great job with her. It's not your fault she's acting out. She just needs some guidance."

"So…" Her sister's voice was full of hope.

"I'll take her." *God help me.*

"You will?"

"Yes. But she should know there will be strict rules. The life of a baker isn't easy and—"

"She'll do it. Trust me. When her father comes home and conveys our rules, she'll agree. Or, at least I hope so. Thanks, sis. I really want to see this turn her life around."

The weight of what Margot was agreeing to rested squarely on her shoulders as they said their goodbyes.

Shining stainless steel counter tops beckoned for their daily dusting of flour as Margot made her way back into the kitchen. She stretched her fingers and donned her apron, turning the stereo on so that classical music wafted from her mounted speakers.

But, just before she dropped the first ingredients into her mixing bowl, she stopped, resting her hands against the cold metal top of her workstation.

What was she doing? Had she lost her mind, agreeing to take in Taylor? The teen was notorious for being a troublemaker, but it was more than that. There was a lot of hurt for her to deal with having lost her mother at age eleven. When Renee married Dillon, Taylor was thirteen and not looking for another mother. Six years and she still hadn't accepted Renee.

Wiping away a stray hair from her shoulder, Margot dropped eggs one at a time into the sugar and milk concoction in the industrial mixer. Maybe the Lord had a bigger use for Margot's spare bedroom than a place to collect the dusty stacks of paperback mysteries she had collected. Maybe it was time to open up her home and her heart to her niece in a way that could bring healing to them both.

∿

"I THOUGHT you were getting that young thing at the airport today."

Margot delivered a steaming caramel pecan cinnamon roll and cup of black coffee to the small, round table where Bentley Anderson, one of her regular customers, sat with newspaper in hand.

"I'm just waiting for Rosie to show up."

"Saw her at the senior center last night," Bentley said taking a sip of his coffee. "She and Betty were tearing it up at the pinochle table."

The corner of Margot's mouth quirked. "Real exciting, I'm sure."

"Hey, watch it, young lady." He stared her down, one bushy eyebrow raised. "Things get exciting over at the senior center. You'd be surprised."

"Don't I know it?" She propped hands on her hips. "I volunteer at least once a month over there. You all are a rambunctious bunch."

"You should bring that niece of yours over."

Margot narrowed her eyes. "You know, that's a good idea."

DANIELLE COLLINS

"I'm full of them." Bentley's laugh was rough and mingled with the sound of bells from the door opening.

"There you are," Margot said, watching as Rosie stepped into the bakery and undid the bright yellow scarf she had tied around her short, gray and black hair.

"It's gusting out there."

"That's not a real word," Bentley said, his gaze fixed on the paper.

"It sure is." Rosie eyed him but turned her attention back to Margot. "Sorry I was late, took a little longer to get going this morning."

Any other morning and Margot wouldn't have even noticed her part-time employee being a few minutes late, but she had at least a thirty-minute drive to Ronald Regan Airport to pick up Taylor and you never knew what traffic was going to be like.

"No problem, but I'm late. You'll be all right?"

Rosie gave her a look. "You *know* I'll be fine, girl. Now go!"

Grinning, Margot grabbed her purse and light jacket from the backroom and rushed out the door to where she'd parked at the end of Main Street in the public parking lot. Pulling onto the freeway, she glanced at her phone, happy to see she hadn't received a text from Taylor yet.

Thankfully, traffic wasn't as bad as she'd expected and she

8

pulled into the pickup line right on time, her eyes scanning for Taylor's blonde hair and lithe frame.

A waving hand caught her attention and she pulled the car over, recognizing Taylor instantly.

"Hello!" Margot said, slipping out of the car with extended hands.

"Hey, Aunt Margot," Taylor said, thin arms wrapping around her.

"We need to feed you some pastries," Margot said, leaning back with a grin. "You're much too thin."

Taylor blushed, her grin widening. "A girl needs to watch her figure if she's going to the beach every day."

"Good thing you won't be spending much time at the beach then." The girl's expression fell and Margot rushed to explain. "It's freezing, Taylor!"

"It's going to be summer," she said, laughing.

"True, but by that time, you'll be elbow deep in dough."

She sent a look to the side, but Margot read it loud and clear. She was *not* happy about the arrangements.

"Let's get your stuff into the car and head back to North Bank. We'll get you settled in the spare bedroom and then I'll take you out for Italian. You do still like Italian food, right?"

"Yeah." Her response was noncommittal but Margot

decided not to let it affect her. Things were going to change, that was a given, but she would make the most of it.

They drove back down I-365, blessedly going against the flow of traffic, and by the time Margot exited the freeway and pulled into the small parking pad in front of her historic row house, Taylor had loosened up, if only a little.

"I remember visiting here."

"That's right. You were…what, fourteen?"

"Yeah." She pulled her backpack from the backseat and Margot picked up her suitcase, dreading the ascent up the steep steps that climbed to the narrow entry way.

"Want some help?"

Hefting the bag, Margot shook her head. "I've got it. I've been taking Krav Maga classes."

"Seriously?" Taylor's eyebrows disappeared into her fringy blonde bangs.

"Hey, your aunt isn't some old lady. I like to stay active. Hiking, biking, baking, and now, self-defense."

Taylor shook her head as Margot hefted the suitcase up and climbed the stone steps. Breathing heavy, she took the inside stairs more slowly until they stood in front of the small guest bedroom.

"I tried my best to stack the crime novels out of the way. I didn't do such a good job."

The girl peered in the room and her eyes widened. "Wow. Have you read all of those?"

Margot surveyed the wall-to-wall bookshelves stacked with crime novels, mysteries, and thrillers. "Not all. A lot of them were Julian's." Margot caught the saddened expression of her niece. "Your uncle was a great man and he loved to read. It always shocked me, knowing that his job as detective put him *in* something like a crime novel every day, but he couldn't get enough of them for some reason. He said he liked to guess 'whodunit' in real life and fiction."

"I miss him."

Her niece's soft words surprised Margot. She and Julian hadn't been around her sister very often. Living on the opposite side of the country did that to a family, but they had made an effort to get to know Renee's husband and his daughter.

"He really liked you."

Taylor turned surprised eyes upward. "Yeah?"

"He didn't call you *mon canard* for nothing."

Taylor laughed. "I never got why he wanted to call me a little duck."

"It was just his way of showing his affection."

"He used to write me letters."

"He did?" Margot felt a rush of warmth flood her chest.

Her husband had been a wonderful, kind, and caring man. It didn't really surprise her that he would have taken a special interest in his sister-in-law's adopted daughter.

"Yeah. It was after we came to visit here. He started sending letters and cards almost every month. I really looked forward to them. I'm sorry...that he's gone."

"Me too, Tay," Margot said, resting her hand on the girl's shoulder. "Hey, why don't you get settled in then we'll go to dinner? The dresser over there is empty and you can hang anything you want in the closet. We'll have to share the bathroom, but I think we'll manage."

Taylor nodded without saying anything and closed the door behind her, leaving Margot in the hall. Thoughts of her late husband squeezed at Margot's heart, but the ache was different than it had been. Five years had gone a long way to heal the brokenness, though the place he'd filled in her life would never be the same again.

CHAPTER 2

*T*aylor emerged from her room forty minutes later looking exhausted but insisting she was hungry. Margot knew the jetlag wouldn't really catch up to her before the morning, but her niece had taken an early flight so she assured her it would be a quick dinner break then to bed for them both.

When they pulled into the small parking lot at the back of *Pane Dolce*, Taylor sent a wary look her way. "Sweet Bread?"

Margot laughed. "I forgot you took Italian in High School. Antonio didn't think anyone would know what it said, at least that's the way he tells it. I always thought he just didn't know what to name his restaurant."

Taylor looked doubtful.

"Despite the name," Margot rushed to assure her, "it's the

best, most authentic Italian cuisine this side of the Atlantic."

"Whatever you say."

They entered through the back door and a large, salt and pepper-haired man rushed up to them with arms held wide. "*Mia bella!*"

"Hello, Antonio," Margot said, kissing both of his cheeks in the traditional greeting. "This is my niece, Taylor. She'll be staying with me for the summer."

"*È molto carina.* She is very pretty. Like her aunt, no?"

Taylor blushed and Margot laughed. "We'd like a table, you old flirt."

"*Sì.* For you, my best table. This way."

They trailed behind him in the busy restaurant and he seated them at a round table in the bay window at the front of the restaurant.

"I feel like we're on display," Taylor muttered under her breath.

"*Sì.* Such beauty cannot be hidden," Antonio said with a devilish grin.

He handed over their menus and promised to return soon to take their order personally. Taylor studied her menu for a moment before putting it down, resting her head in the palm of her hand, eyes on the crowd in the large, dimly lit room.

"You okay?" Margot asked, putting down her own menu.

"Yeah. Missing my friends, I guess."

"Oh?"

Taylor shot her a look. "I know. Renee probably told you that I hang out with a bunch of deadbeats, but they really aren't bad guys. And, no matter what Renee thinks—I'm *not* doing drugs, Aunt Marg."

The words stole Margot's breath. She didn't want to speak against Renee or incite the girl's anger. It was dangerous territory that Margot wanted to tread carefully. Then again, the first night Taylor was in Virginia and during their first meal—in public no less—probably wasn't the time to have a serious conversation with her.

"Your mom cares about you," she said, hoping the use of 'mom' wouldn't offend the girl. "She's just worried."

"Yeah. Whatever."

Margot was about to press the point when a waiter showed up with a pitcher of water. He was young, likely in his early twenties, and had a flashy smile pointed toward Taylor.

"*Buonasera*, lovely ladies. Can I get you something to drink besides water?"

Margot fought the urge to wave a hand in front of his face as if to remind him that she was there as well, but it wasn't worth the effort.

"Water's fine," she said.

"And you?"

Margot imagined she could see the hormones flying between the two and fought the urge to roll her eyes. Ah, to be nineteen again. She cringed at the reality though, knowing she wouldn't wish to go back to that tenuous time.

"Water's good," Taylor said, her smile sliding into place with the perfect amount of flirtation.

Margot cleared her throat and the young man took a step back, his own smile a match to Taylor's, before he disappeared. It was looking like Margot would have her work cut out for her keeping track of Taylor.

Once their order was taken, the over-eager water boy visited their table no less than five times in the span of twenty minutes. Margot was about to call Antonio over to have him say something to his server when Taylor bolted up from the table, her napkin falling to the floor in her haste.

"I'm, uh, going to the bathroom." She forced a smile at Margot then turned toward the back of the restaurant.

Margot watched her go, wondering at her odd behavior, then straightened in her seat when she saw the same server trailing behind her niece.

"It's just a coincidence," she said to herself just as Antonio walked up to the table.

"Is everything *bene*—good?"

"Yes. *Sì*. It is wonderful, as always." Margot hesitated, then, after one more glance toward the back of the restaurant, turned toward Antonio. "Who's the server who's been helping us? Filling our water and such."

"Ack." Antonio rolled his eyes. "He's a friend of my sister's kid. Marco Rossario. Word on the street is that he's bad news, but you know me, *mia bella*, I'm a...what do they say? Softie? He's only just started working here—if you call making eyes at every girl under the age of thirty working."

Margot glanced at her watch. Taylor had been gone too long.

"I—um, excuse me for a moment. The washroom?" she asked, pointing to the back.

Antonio smiled and pointed toward the back where Taylor had disappeared. The thought of Marco being anywhere near Taylor sent a chill down Margot's spine as she rounded the corner that led toward the bathrooms.

"Stop it! Seriously!" Margot instantly knew the firm, somewhat high-pitched voice belonging to Taylor.

But where was she? The hall ended in a door to the men's bathroom and a door to the left to the women's. Then there was—the closet!

"I said I don't have—"

17

Margot yanked open the door to find Taylor pressed up against the side of a utility closet, Marco holding both of her wrists by the side of her head.

"Hey!" Margot said. "Get away from her!"

Tears filled Taylor's eyes and she took Marco's distracted attention to yank her arms away and shove him against the other side of the wall. In a crash of mops and supplies, he fell backward, not quite catching himself before he fell to the floor.

Margot could tell that Taylor was shaking from head to toe and she wrapped her arm around the girl, directing her back toward the main restaurant area and the back door. Antonio came toward them, his eyes wide at seeing Taylor's tear-streaked face.

"What has happened?" He looked between Taylor and Margot.

"Marco Rossario attacked my niece." Margot felt the anger surge up in her at the thought of him taking advantage of Taylor like he had. Taylor had likely gotten herself into the situation with flirtation, but it didn't excuse the fact that he had tried to force himself on her.

"Shall I call the police?" Antonio looked to Taylor, waiting for her instruction.

"Just—just forget it. I want to go home." Taylor wrapped her arms around her middle.

Antonio looked helplessly to Margot and she nodded. "I think we should leave. Can we take our meal to go?"

"Of course! I will wrap it up personally. And you are not to worry—I will let Marco go this moment!"

Without waiting for their confirmation, he left them to get their meals and Margot turned to Taylor. "I'm sorry, honey. Are you going to be all right? Do you want to talk to the police?"

"Nah." Taylor pushed hair from her face. "I...I don't know what was going on. I just want to go back to your place."

Margot felt the weight of exhaustion and worry taking over. Taking care of Taylor was going to be a lot more challenging than she'd expected. What was the right thing to do in this situation?

"Maybe we *should* call the police."

"No." Taylor met her gaze, eyes fierce. "I seriously just want to go back to your house. I'm so done with today."

Worry still pressing in on her, Margot nodded and they made their way to the back where Antonio met them with a large paper sack.

"Here is your dinner and I added a piece of my famous tiramisu. It will not match up to your confections, *mia bella,* but I hope it is a sweet ending to a not so sweet day." He looked worriedly at Taylor then back at Margot, who patted him on the shoulder.

"Thank you, Antonio. It's not your fault."

He nodded. "Thank you. But he is gone. I have fired him. Please, do come back soon."

Margot nodded and the women walked out into the fading evening light. She clicked her key fob and the car beeped back just as a shape emerged from the darkness of the alley behind the restaurant. Taylor gasped and latched on to Margot's sleeve as Marco's face became clear to them both.

"Dude, seriously. Leave me alone!" Taylor said.

"Hey, I just want the—" he began, but when he got too close, Taylor lunged forward and shoved him away with both hands.

"Stay. Away!" she screamed.

Margot was stunned by the action and her scream as much as Marco was, but he caught himself before falling over just as the back door opened. His eyes were wide as they darted to a young couple exiting with a to-go box in hand.

"Whoa," Marco said, holding up his hands.

"I swear, if you don't get out of here..." Taylor was seething in rage now and Margot placed her hand on the girl's arm.

"You need to leave," Margot said, stepping between her niece and the young man.

He opened his mouth as if he was going to say something then closed it and ran off behind the alley. Taylor was shaking again and Margot felt her own heart pounding. The couple stared at them wide-eyed, but Margot flashed a fake smile their way.

They looked between her and where Marco had run off, but Margot didn't wait for them to say anything. "Come on, honey, let's go."

Once she and Taylor were in the car, she locked it and looked over at the young woman. She was visibly shaken and Margot's heart broke.

"Are you all right?"

Taylor gave a short nod.

"I think we should call the police."

"No!" Taylor looked at Margot with fear and apprehension hiding behind her blue-eyed gaze. "Please. Let's just go home. I...I want to go to bed."

Margot looked at her for another moment before turning on the car. This was not how she'd envisioned her first night with Taylor going, but at least the boy had left them alone and Taylor was safe. But, despite her niece's protest about calling the police, Margot planned to put in a call the next day to a friend on the force. If nothing else, at least she could give him a heads up that there was a volatile young man on the loose in their small community.

CHAPTER 3

*T*hree o'clock came earlier than normal—or at least it felt that way the next day as Margot unlocked the shop door and flipped on the lights. The scent of Lysol and lemons greeted her and she smiled. Every time Rosie worked, she cleaned as if *The Parisian Pâtisserie* was a hospital, not a bakery. Then again, clean was better than dirty.

Dumping her large purse on her desk and flipping the switch to start the coffee, she thought about Taylor, still asleep in her guest bedroom. After the night they'd had, she decided to give the girl a day to adjust to the new time zone as well as living in her small row home. It was a rude awakening to anyone when they started work at a bakery and needed to be ready to go as early as three.

Besides, the way Taylor had looked when they got back, she wasn't sure if the girl would be able to sleep at all. It was difficult, having someone in your care. Granted,

Taylor was nineteen and an adult, but Margot still felt responsible for her.

Pushing up her sleeves and turning on her classical music, she began several projects at once, making sure the dough that needed to rise was set to go ahead of schedule today. She worked diligently and by the time seven o'clock rolled around, she was ready to open her doors.

The morning crowd didn't usually show up until eight, thanks to the high percentage of senior citizens living in North Bank, but there was always the chance that someone on their way to work would stop in for breakfast or a cup of coffee or both.

One look out the front door and she knew she'd have a few minutes to spare. Remembering her promise to herself, she picked up her phone and scrolled through her contacts.

There, resting under the As, was the name she was looking for: Adam Eastwood.

With the name came a rush of memories. Adam, lead detective on the police force in North Bank, had known her husband Julian back when they'd been on the police force in New York. The connection had only been made after Julian's death and the new detective who had filled his shoes made a point to come introduce himself to Julian's widow.

Even still, it boggled her mind that they had known one another and that Adam was now doing Julian's previous job, but either way, she saw it as a blessing. They had fallen into an easy friendship and he was a connection—albeit small—to the friends she'd made when Julian was alive.

Biting her lip, she tapped his number and the phone buzzed to life.

"Margot?"

"Hi, Adam." She took in a breath. Was she really going to do this?

The memory of the anger and fear on Taylor's face resurfaced. The young man might be gone from *Pane Dolce*, but that didn't mean he still couldn't cause trouble in their small town.

"Wow. It's been a while. Uh, what's up?" Adam's easygoing tone did nothing to hide his curiosity.

"I had something I wanted to mention to you. Kind of under the radar." Was she going about this the right way? Or would Adam think she was taking advantage of their friendship?

"What's that? Everything all right?"

She relayed the incident from the night before ending with, "I didn't like the look in Marco's eyes. I just... I don't know. If Julian were alive, he would tell me to follow my gut." She laughed imagining him saying that to her now. "So I am."

Adam's silence spoke volumes. Did he think she was over stepping? Being a worrywart?

"Did you say Marco Rossario?" His tone was rock hard, all manner of friendliness gone. It was a tone she'd heard Julian take on before—when he was on a case.

"Yes," she said tentatively.

"Oh, Margot." His tone sent a shiver coursing down her spine. "Marco Rossario was found dead by the river this morning."

THE LATE SPRING sunlight shone through bright, puffy clouds as Margot rushed down the sidewalk toward the police station. She'd left Rosie in charge of the bakery and, after a phone call to make sure that Taylor was doing all right, she'd set off for the station and a meeting with Adam.

It had been his idea. A purely informational meeting and one that she'd convinced him to leave Taylor out of, for now, but she had a sneaking suspicion that her niece would need to have a conversation with the detective as well.

A uniformed officer opened the door for her as he was leaving and nodded. She thought she'd seen him before but he was focused and barely took notice of her. After she checked in at the front desk, she took a seat and waited for Adam.

The station held all types of memories for her. Of coming to work with Julian for a spouse luncheon. Helping him decide on the perfect photo to hang to the right of his door, one that would always remind him of his home in France. Bringing him lunch when he'd forgotten it on the counter—that had happened more times than she could remember.

Sighing, she re-crossed her legs and focused her attention out the bright front windows. During those days, she had stayed at home, writing for an online news outlet. It had been fun, mentally invigorating work, but her bakery now was the fulfillment of a lifetime of dreams. If only Julian could have seen *The Parisian Pâtisserie*.

"Margot."

She turned to see Adam in the doorway. He cut an impressive profile at 6'3" with broad shoulders pulling the sleeves of his suit coat tight. He looked good. She'd always thought him a handsome man.

"Adam Eastwood. It's good to see you."

He grinned and came forward, giving her a light hug. "You too. Come on back with me. You remember the way."

She did. All too well. It was a shame that Julian and Adam had never been able to work together in North Bank.

They walked down a dingy hall, the same ugly green color as it had been all those years ago, and he showed her into his office. Since they had rearranged things in the department, it wasn't the same office as Julian's but it was similar, flooding her with memories.

"Please, take a seat."

She did and folded her hands in her lap. "How are you, Adam?"

He seemed to allow the momentary distraction from the reason why she was there and shrugged. "Busy. Too busy."

"Oh?"

"Not with anything town-related, exactly. I don't know if you remember, but my brother is a detective up in D.C. They've had some interesting cases recently and, because of my unique background, I've been called in to consult on a few. It means making the trip up to the big city almost every weekend—if not more—but it's interesting work."

"I do remember you mentioning Anthony was in D.C. How exciting for you."

"Something like that," he said with a grin. "But it's taken me away from North Bank a lot and…friends."

His gaze held hers and she wondered briefly if he included her in that circle of friends. But the thought of young Marco Rossario dead grounded her again.

"About Marco," she said, leaning forward.

"Right." Adam shuffled some papers around and then considered her. "So you say your niece got into an argument with him last night at *Pane Dolce*?"

Margot recounted what had happened. "I asked her if I should call the police, I even considered it after she turned me down, but she was insistent. She just wanted to go home. I just didn't like the look in his eye when he came up to her in the parking lot."

She thought back. His behavior had been strange. Almost as if he were asking Taylor for something—but how could that be possible? Taylor had only just come to North Bank. It had to be something else.

"I've been down to see Antonio and he shed some light on who Marco is exactly."

"A friend of Lorenzo's, or so I heard," Margot said.

"Exactly. I guess Carmela is vising her parents in Italy from now until the end of summer and her son has been staying in her house with Marco. I couldn't find Lorenzo to question, though."

Margot shifted back in her seat, mind going over what she knew of the Bianchi family. "Did Antonio know anything about Marco? I mean, aside from his friendship with his nephew?"

Adam's eyes narrowed and he leaned forward, elbows on the desk. "Why the interest, Margot?"

She laughed, sending him a smile. "You should know by now that I love a puzzle. Though, the death of a young man is much more than a puzzle of course."

Adam nodded. "I remember Julian telling me you liked to poke your nose into his cases."

"He did?" Her eyebrows rose at this news. She hadn't known that her husband had been in contact with Adam after he had moved from New York.

"We stayed in touch. He had many things to tell me about you." Adam's grin made a dimple appear and she felt her stomach clench at what he could mean. "But no. To answer your question, Antonio said he knew next to nothing about the boy. He'd hired him for the main fact that his other busboy had gone home for the summer and he was short a pair of hands."

"How…" She grimaced. "How did he die?"

"We found him at the base of the Miller's Bridge."

Margot's mind filled in the details of the old bridge that ran across South Fork, an offshoot of the Potomac River. It was a deep, rocky, and treacherous portion of the river.

"Are you thinking it was a suicide?"

"It's…inconclusive." He hesitated.

"Was he…pushed then?" She swallowed, the idea making her feeling nauseous.

"You know that's confidential," Adam said, pulling out

another sheet of paper. He eyed her. "But I don't know that it would hurt to tell you. He was stabbed."

Her eyes widened.

"We don't have the murder weapon yet, but I'm fairly confident that was his cause of death, not the fall."

Margot paled. A murder in North Bank.

He shrugged and folded the report closed. "I only told you this to assuage your curiosity and because you're a friend. Don't you go telling anyone." He fixed a hard stare on her.

"I wouldn't." She raised her hands in defense.

"I know." He held her gaze for a moment longer.

Margot resisted the urge to press him for more details—why, she wasn't exactly sure. The poor boy's fate was sad indeed and Adam would do a fine job investigating it. Maybe it was just that old habits died hard. She missed having Julian to talk to about his cases. Mystery books aside, real life was much more unpredictable. Maybe she was more like her late husband than even she realized.

"Well, thank you, Adam. I won't take up any more of your time. Besides, I've got to get back to Rosie. Who knows what trouble she'll get herself in."

Adam gave her his signature, easy-going smile. "You tell Rosie Mae I said hello."

Standing, Margot considered him for a moment. "Come

to the bakery some time and you can tell her that yourself."

"I just might do that." She turned but paused at the door when he called out to her. "I'll need to speak with Taylor too."

The words sunk in with a zap of apprehension. "I thought you might."

"Can I come by tonight? Maybe she'll feel more comfortable if we talk at your place."

Margot considered this and knew that would be true. Despite the fact she wanted to shelter Taylor from all of this, she knew Adam was just doing his job.

"Yes. Come by around seven and we can have dessert."

"If we're talking about your baked goods, I'm there."

She merely smiled and left the office, showing herself out. The sun still shone brightly, but dark storm clouds gathered on the horizon and Margot couldn't help but think of it as a warning.

CHAPTER 4

*T*aylor pulled dishes from the table, simultaneously checking messages on her phone every few seconds. By the amount of texts she was getting, she was certainly popular. She'd seemed to recover from the previous night well, though Margot wasn't sure how she would take the news about Marco.

Glancing at the clock for the third time in the same minute, Margot knew she should have told Taylor about the expected visitor. It was nine minutes until seven o'clock and her stomach was twisted in knots.

"Taylor, I probably should have mentioned this before," she said, waiting until the girl looked up from her phone, "but my friend Detective Adam Eastwood is going to be stopping by in a few minutes. He, uh, he has some questions for...us."

Taylor blinked. "A detective? Questions? What are you talking about, Aunt Margot?"

Here was the moment of truth. "I phoned him this morning to relay the incident from last night at Antonio's place—"

"I asked you not to call the police," Taylor interrupted.

"I know, but I thought it best to warn him there was a disruptive man in our community. We're very tightknit with a big population of senior citizens. I feel responsible to watch out for them."

"Okay. Whatever. But *why* is he coming here?"

"That's just it," she said, twisting a dishtowel in her hands. "Marco Rossario, the young man from last night, he was found dead this morning."

Taylor paled at the news, her hand reaching out to steady herself on the nearest chair. "Dead? Did he, like, have an accident or what?"

"No, sweetie." Margot tried to break the news as calmly as possible. "He was murdered."

"Whoa." Taylor put a hand to her stomach and Margot prayed she wouldn't be sick. "I—I can't believe that. How? What happened?"

"Well—" A light knock sounded at the door and she shrugged. "That'll be Adam. Why don't you have a seat in the living room?"

Taylor nodded, staring down as she walked like she was processing the information she'd just gotten. And why shouldn't she be? It wasn't every day that you were around someone one day and they were gone the next.

"Hi, Adam," she said, opening the door to let her friend in.

"You doing all right?" he asked, pulling a baseball cap from his head. He'd changed out of the gray suit he'd worn that morning and now wore jeans and a plain black t-shirt. It tugged at his shoulders, showing muscular arms and proving he was more than fit for his job.

"I suppose. I just told Taylor about what had happened. Maybe it wasn't the best timing, but I didn't want to spoil dinner."

He offered a sad smile. "It'll be all right. You're doing great."

"No, I actually think I'm the world's worst aunt." She wrapped her arms around herself and shook her head. "I mean, a murder? In our town? And my sister thought it was a good idea to send Taylor here?"

"Hey." Adam reached out and rested a hand on her arm, squeezing gently. "You're doing the best you can. Besides, you had no control over this. Let's go have dessert and I'll talk with her. Don't worry, I'll make it as painless for her as possible."

"Okay." Margot led the way into the living room where Taylor was curled up on the couch, staring out the window with her phone forgotten beside her. "Hey, sweetie, this is my friend Detective—"

"You can call me Adam," he interjected. "You must be Taylor. I saw pictures of you as a kid. You've definitely grown."

She offered a weak smile and Adam sat down on the chair across from her.

"I'm going to grab some macaroons."

Adam flashed her a smile then began talking to Taylor again. Margot couldn't hear the conversation from the kitchen, but she sent up a prayer that it wouldn't completely frighten Taylor and that they'd still be able to get past this and have an enjoyable summer. Somehow.

"Yes!" Adam said when she came back into the room. "These are my favorite. Taylor, have you had your aunts macaroons before?"

Taylor shook her head but reached out for a chocolate hazelnut macaroon just as Adam grabbed the lemon. Margot selected her favorite, lavender and vanilla, and they munched on the airy French cookies for a moment before Adam spoke again.

"So, after he slipped you the note—"

"What note?" Margot interrupted. At Taylor's guilty look, she turned to Adam for an explanation then back to Taylor when he looked at her.

35

"He slipped me a note," she said, looking down at her cookie. "I mean, do you really think he needed to refill our waters so many times?"

"What did the note say?" Margot's tone came out harsher than she'd intended.

"Chill, Aunt Margot. He just wanted to talk with me. You know, ask me for my number or something. I didn't think it would hurt to talk with him."

"So you went to talk with him?" Adam asked, a small notebook in his hand where he jotted down notes.

"Yeah. He wasn't interested in talking, though." She blushed and looked out the window.

"So that's when your aunt found you guys in the closet?"

Something passed over Taylor's face, but she nodded. "Yeah."

Adam looked to Margot then back at Taylor. "You didn't give him your number or anything, right?"

Taylor looked down at her macaroon. "No."

Adam made another note then leaned forward to snatch another cookie.

"Look, I'm tired. Can I go to bed? Aunt Margot's going to get me up before dawn and I really should get some sleep."

Margot fought for composure, shocked that the girl was

thinking of bed at seven-twenty in the evening, but she looked to Adam to make sure he was done with his questions.

"Sure," he said, folding the notepad closed and stowing it in his jacket pocket.

She shuffled past them, bypassing the macaroon plate and disappearing down the hall until they heard her door close.

"Huh," he said, his eyes searching the empty space in front of him.

"What?"

He met her gaze and frowned. "What?"

"When Julian used to 'huh,' it always meant something wasn't lining up."

Adam offered her a half-smile. "Are you psychoanalyzing me?"

She leaned back, savoring the last bite of her macaroon before answering him. "I wouldn't dream of it, *Detective*. I'm just a baker after all."

He held her gaze for a moment before pushing to his feet. "I've got to get going. I may not have baker's hours, but I do have a lot of work ahead of me. Thanks for letting me come by tonight."

Margot stood as well, wondering just how far she should

push. She could tell he was keeping something from her, but she didn't know what—or if she even had the leverage to demand the information.

"Macaroon for the road?"

"Absolutely." He took another lemon and grinned, taking a bite. "Delicious."

"Come by the bakery any time, Adam. There's more where that came from."

He held her gaze for a moment longer than necessary then turned toward the door. "I may do just that."

∼

"No, a little thinner. Yes, there you go." Margot instructed Taylor on how to make her famous chocolate-filled croissants as the clock raced toward seven o'clock and their opening time. Taylor was already yawning, but she'd get her second wind soon—that or Margot would be giving her another cup of coffee with an extra shot of espresso.

The timer dinged and she reached for the oven door, pulling out more macaroons. Their sweet scent wafted through the kitchen and mingled with the classical music, which Taylor had complained about at first.

Now, though, she hummed along to an aria that had a familiar and repetitive melody. Margot resisted the urge to tell her niece 'I told you so' and instead worked on whipping up the fillings for her macaroons.

By the time Bentley came in, the small bell chiming his presence, she felt well ahead of schedule. His caramel pecan cinnamon roll and cup of coffee delivered, she eyed the newspaper in his hand.

"Anything…interesting in there?"

"You betcha there is."

Margot's stomach clenched. "Oh?" Knowing ahead of time about a murder in town wasn't something she wanted to gloat about.

"Sure thing. There's some controversy about putting a halt to the construction on the new senior center lodge. I'm *irate, seething,* one could even say *apoplectic.*"

"You've been doing crosswords again—that or reading the thesaurus I gave you for Christmas."

Bentley grinned up at her, his bristly moustache tipping up at the corners. "A little bit of both. But it's true."

This wasn't the news she'd expected, but she decided to go along with it anyway. "Why would they do that?"

He sighed heavily, leaning back and slurping from his coffee cup. "Darn politics. That's why."

"Politics?"

"Forget I said anything. We're working on it."

She knew by 'we' he meant he and other patrons that frequented the senior center. They were a rowdy bunch.

"All I know is that I wouldn't be caught dead on the wrong side of you all." She laughed but noticed his expression had turned serious.

"Speaking of dead," he said, conspiratorially, "A body was found at the river near Miller's Bridge."

So the news *had* made the paper. "Oh?" she said, trying to look surprised.

His eyes narrowed. "What do *you* know about it?"

"Me?" she feigned surprise. "I—I don't know..." She wasn't willing to lie to her friend, though she didn't want Taylor to be caught up in the middle of a scandal like this. Somehow, mentioning what happened at Antonio's restaurant opened her up for questions as well.

"Come on, tell old Bentley. I'm an old man. Who would I tell?" He grinned at her, his eyebrows wagging.

"You'd tell the entire senior center, who would somehow tell the rest of the town." She crossed her arms, daring him to contradict her.

"All right, so you may have a point there. Speaking of, you're coming tonight, right?"

"Coming..." Margot searched her memory for what was going on that night.

"It's World Dinner Night. You promised to bring French pastries."

"Oh," she gasped, a hand flying to cover her mouth, "With Taylor coming and all of this—" His look said, *I knew you had something to tell.* "I completely forgot."

"Good thing I'm here every morning to remind you of your commitments. Besides, bring the kid. We like to see a little life in that place every now and again. You know, someone under the age of fifty."

"Hey," Margot said, nailing him with a look.

"Present company excluded." Bentley gave a rasping laugh and looked back to his newspaper. "Besides, then you can tell me—and everyone else—what you know about this murder."

Spinning on her heel, she walked back toward the kitchen to avoid having to say anything else about what she knew —or didn't know—about the murder.

"What was he saying about tonight?" Taylor asked. Flour dusted her cheek and her lopsided ponytail was sliding closer to her neck than the top of her head.

"World Dinner Night."

"What is that?" she turned back to the dough she was kneading and Margot had to bite back her criticism of her technique. They would be the toughest loaves of bread to ever come out of her shop.

"Every third Tuesday of the month they do World Dinner Night at the senior center. Different restaurants around the area usually provide entrées or side dishes from different cultural backgrounds. I'm often called upon to bring French pastries. They open the event up to the community. You pay a small fee and get to enjoy the meal with the seniors. They are a crafty bunch when it comes to raising money, especially for the new building they are putting up—well, hopefully." Margot thought of the article Bentley had mentioned. She had thought they were close to their funding goal, but Bentley made it sound like they weren't. If so, where had the money gone?

"Are we going to go?"

Drawn from her thoughts, Margot looked at her niece. "Do you want to go?"

"I don't know." Taylor shrugged. "It kind of sounds fun."

Feeling like she could have been knocked over by a feather, Margot feigned surprise. "All right. Yes. We'll go."

"Sweet."

Taylor went back to kneading the life out of the dough and Margot slipped into baker mode as she thought of the desserts she would need to make for that night. Familiar recipes, ingredient lists, and baking times filled her head, but soon they were sifted to the side as she thought again about the poor boy that had been killed. It was awful to think of anyone dying, but the fact that she'd seen him the night before stuck with her.

There had to be a logical explanation. She thought of Antonio and what he might know. Would he be at World Dinner Night tonight? He often brought some of his favorite Italian meals to share. If so, she would make a point to talk with him.

But, for now, she had to focus on baking or the seniors would likely rebel.

CHAPTER 5

"*S*o, it's like a fundraiser?" Taylor took a moment to look up from her phone long enough to show Margot just how excited she *wasn't* about attending the dinner that night before her eyes sought out the next text message.

"Yes and no." Margot maneuvered the car onto a side street shaded by large trees and began looking for a parking spot. She had a feeling the lot would be full plus she liked to leave the closer spots for the elderly. Finding an empty spot, she pulled in. "They are raising money to put up a new senior center lodge, as they are calling it. The old one is falling apart and they want to tear it down and put up a new one. They see it as future income for them, renting it out for parties, weddings, and the like, plus they want it to be more handicap accessible. It's really a great thing they're doing."

"Sure." Taylor was distracted by her phone again.

Part of Margot wanted to snatch the device away and tell her niece that it was time to grow up and start having face-to-face conversations with those around her, but she bit her cheek and prayed for strength. Getting after Taylor only a few days after she'd arrived wasn't the best way to approach something that probably had deeper strings in Taylor's life.

"Hey," Margot said. The tone of her voice was serious enough to draw the young woman's gaze. "I know it's not easy being here and I'm sure spending the evening with a bunch of senior citizens isn't high on your list of things to do, but these are great people. I've gotten to know them and they hold a special place in my heart. I guess..." She fumbled for the words under the weight of the young woman's gaze. "I just hope you could, you know, try to get to know them."

"Yeah. Sure." She slipped the phone into her purse and reached for the handle. "Ready?"

Margot almost laughed. The better question was if Taylor was ready for what she was about to walk into. Instead, she nodded and opened her own door.

They walked down Front Street and took the walkway leading around the building to the front entrance. There was already a short line forming and she waved to Sally and another woman Margot hadn't talked to much as they accepted payment for the dinner. When they got to the front of the line, Sally winked up at her.

"Lynellen, this here is the mastermind behind those wonderful French pastries!"

The other woman's eyes grew round. "Mercy. You don't say! Well, honey, you should go in for free because I think half of the folks who are coming today have mentioned those pastries."

Margot shook her head. "Absolutely not. If we're going to get the lodge built, we'll need every penny." She handed over ten dollars and introduced Taylor to the women then walked around the table and entered the dated center.

Light fixtures circa the nineteen-sixties hung across the room, more than a few bulbs burned out. It created a mood-lighting affect, even though she wasn't sure that was what they were going for. The green carpet had seen better days and the walls that had once been white were now a dull grayish color.

"Wow. You weren't kidding when you said they needed a new place."

Margot sent her a look that said, *I told you*. "They should be close to their goal, but I haven't heard updates. Except..." She recalled the conversation she'd had with Bentley.

"Yeah?" Taylor's eyebrows were raised.

"Oh, it's probably nothing. One of my customers said that something was going on. Maybe— Oh look, there's Mayor Penberthy."

"Who?"

Margot drew her attention back to her niece, who looked pale. "The mayor. He's over there talking to— Tay, why do you look like you've seen a ghost?"

"I—uh, never mind."

The girl's reaction was strange, but just then Bentley came up, smile widening as he took both of them in with outstretched arms.

"And look who we have here. The famous pastry chef and her budding new assistant. Happy to have you ladies here."

Taylor still looked distracted, but Bentley immediately drew them toward a table and began asking questions about what they wanted to eat. He was thoroughly enjoying his role as a waiter.

"Aren't you quite the host," she observed. "I should hire you part time at the *Pâtisserie,* but I have a feeling you'd eat more than you'd sell, Bentley."

His smile widened. "I'd be delighted. You could just pay me in pastries."

"I somehow don't think it would be equal."

He shrugged and said he'd be right back with their meals. Nearly the moment he was gone the mayor stepped into the spot he had vacated. "Why if it isn't my favorite baker!" His grin made the extra skin under his jaw jiggle slightly and his bushy white eyebrows wagged as if waiting for her to deny his statement.

"Mayor Penberthy, good to see you."

"And who is this lovely lady? Surely not your sister?"

Taylor shifted nervously next to her, but Margot laughed off his comment. "You charmer. This is my niece Taylor."

"Pleased to meet you." He clasped his hands in front of him. "But, Margot, you must tell me the secret to what makes your croissants so amazing."

"Now, Mayor," she laughed, shaking her head. "If I told you that, then you'd have no reason to come by the shop as often as you do."

He placed a hand on his ample stomach and gave a hearty laugh. "You've got me dead to rights there."

"Excuse me," Taylor said, fumbling with her purse while pushing the chair back from the table. "Restroom."

Margot watched her go, concern flashing through her mind.

"You enjoy your dinner now, all right?" The mayor patted her arm and then moved to the next table. He was no doubt garnering votes for the upcoming election. She'd seen him at every community hosted event over the last several months. And when not there, he was often stopping by the *Pâtisserie* for one—or more—of her croissants.

"See you were chatting with Mayor Penberthy." Bentley set their plates of food down with a scowl.

"Have a seat, Bentley. I have a feeling there's a story behind that scowl."

"Where's the kid?"

Margot looked around again, her gaze traveling to the bathrooms on the other side of the room. "Restroom."

He nodded and took a seat next to her. "Remember I was talking about the lodge funds at the shop today?"

"Of course. You were saying it was something political. Surely you don't mean…"

"Before you go getting yourself up in arms, let me give it to you straight. We're missing money."

Margot blinked. "Missing…you mean for the lodge?"

"Yeah." He looked around, rubbing his jaw, the sound of scraping whiskers matching his irritation. "We've got a young whippersnapper handling the funds for us and he says I've lost my marbles—granted, he's not the first to say that—but I've kept track of the money we've gotten and I *know* what he's showing us for totals is not accurate."

"You're taking into account food costs and—"

"Most of it's donated."

He had a point there. Margot frowned, her mind racing to

catch up to the full extent of what he was telling her. "You think... Wait, what does this have to do with the mayor?"

Bentley looked at the mayor then back at her. He was quiet so long she almost wasn't sure he was going to answer. "Mayor Penberthy's campaign has exploded over the last few months. He's raised more support than I thought was possible, considering not a whole lot of folks like him in this town, and it just doesn't sit well with me."

"You think he's stealing money from the senior center."

"I don't have any proof, mind you." Bentley leaned closer. "They think I'm some old man off his rocker, but I aim to get to the bottom of this."

Margot's mind reeled at what Bentley had said. He rushed off to take care of another table, but her thoughts stuck on his words. If Mayor Penberthy *was* taking some of the senior center money, how was he doing that? Who was the young man in charge of the accounts? And how did the mayor think he could get away with it? Per campaign rules, he would have to divulge where his backing was coming from. He couldn't simply claim an extra twenty thousand dollars had just appeared in his account.

If it was possible, maybe she could get together with Bentley and they could comprise a list of what he remembered from their donations from the last several months. She'd been there at many of them and they could easily guess how many had attended, multiply it by what was charged per head, and come up with a tentative number.

Then again, no one kept good track at these events. Having Lynellen and Sally at the front desk was helpful, but they weren't the kind to keep track. Bentley seemed to be the only one who'd noticed the missing money. Though, how no one noticed a large sum of money missing boggled her mind. Then again, if it hadn't happened all at once, it could explain a gradual decrease that didn't alarm anyone.

She trailed her finger over her napkin, lost in thought, until she realized just how long Taylor had been gone.

Frowning, she stood and made her way toward the bathrooms. An image of the night before rushed into her mind. But no, Marco Rossario wouldn't be cornering her niece; he was dead.

A chill rushed through her at the same time as a wave of sadness. If he really had been stabbed, that meant a murder in North Bank and that meant there was a murderer on the loose. How would she explain this to Taylor—let alone her sister?

At the women's restroom door, she knocked and called out. "Taylor, honey, are you in there?"

There was no response.

Margot's heart began to beat more loudly and she called out to her niece again without response. She was just about to try the handle when a commotion at the front of the center drew her attention.

There, surrounded by several uniformed officers, stood Adam. His gaze was fixed on Margot and she felt the air leave her lungs as he paced toward her, the determination in his steps. The look on his face betrayed any hope she'd had of his visit bearing good news.

"Margot," he said, the strain in his words sending off red warning lights in her mind. "Where's Taylor?"

"T-Taylor?" Her mind suddenly felt sluggish and she blinked to clear it. "I—I don't know. She came to the bathroom, but I've called out to her and she hasn't answered. I was about to go in…"

"Please, stand back." She watched in horror as Adam instructed a female officer to come forward. She knocked once and then, trying the handle, found it locked.

"Sir?" she asked.

Adam nodded and she stepped back as one of the other officers strode forward and kicked at the door. After a few kicks, the frame cracked and the door swung inward to reveal an empty bathroom, curtains blowing in the wind through the open window.

Margot looked to Adam. "She's gone."

THE COOL NIGHT air rushed over Margot's skin as she raced outside behind Adam. Her heart thudded in her chest and she felt a sickening knot tighten in her stomach. Not only was Adam—a police detective—looking for her niece, but her niece wasn't where she said she was going to be.

What was going on?

"Harver, Jackson, you search that way. Collier and Smith, you go to the left." The officers nodded and broke off in unison.

"You should stay here, Margot." Adam's expression could have been carved in granite.

"No, I can help you find her."

He looked as if he were ready to argue with her, but then nodded instead. "Stay right behind me."

She nodded and followed as they went toward the parking lot. Where would Taylor go? Why had she run in the first place? Better yet, why was Adam looking for her?

Margot wanted to ask all of her questions at once, but she knew now was not the time. Adam was focused and she remembered when Julian had gotten that way. The last thing he wanted to do was talk. Just like her late husband, Adam was a man of action—it was what made them both such talented detectives. They thought things through, but then they acted on those thoughts.

She followed as he ran through the parking lot, then he skidded to a halt and she nearly ran into him.

"Where did you park?"

"Down the street—I never park in the lot if I can help it."

He nodded. "Show me."

Adrenaline coursing through her, she nodded and turned toward the street. They jogged down a block and she spotted her car ahead, at least one more block away. Another car was double parked next to it, facing away from them. What was going on?

"Margot—" Adam said, his tone warning. "Get behind me."

"That's my—"

"I see it." His words were as sharp as steel. "Get behind."

She did and he picked up his pace. They were still five car-lengths away when the person standing at the second car's window stood up.

Taylor.

Margot gasped just as the car's brake lights disappeared and the back tires squealed in protest at being forced into movement without warning.

"No!" Adam yelled before kicking up into a fast run.

Taylor flattened herself against Margot's car, looking frightened as Adam chased through the burning tire smoke after the car. He returned almost immediately, jaw clenched.

"They got away." Then his gaze nailed Taylor. "Who was that?"

"I—I don't know. Just s-someone asking for directions."

He leaned closer, as if daring her to lie to his face. But was she lying? Margot had the uneasy feeling she was, but she couldn't be sure. And wasn't she supposed to be on her niece's side?

Adam radioed in to the other officers to give them their location, then he pulled out handcuffs from his pocket.

Margot felt the blood drain from her face. "What is this about?"

"It's a precaution."

"She's not dangerous, Adam," Margot snapped.

His eyes shifted and he seemed suddenly uneasy. There was something he wasn't telling her. Something about Taylor.

"What is going on?" Margot demanded.

He met her gaze. "I'm sorry, Margot, but..." He ran a hand through his hair, glancing to Taylor with narrowed eyes. "We found the murder weapon."

Cold dread spread through Margot.

"Taylor's prints were on the knife."

"What? You've got to be kidding! You think I killed Marco? No way! I just *got* here. Why would I kill him?"

Margot shot Adam a look and wrapped her arm around Taylor's shoulders. "Quiet, honey. This has to be some mistake."

Three officers arrived on the scene and another drove a squad car up the next moment, the blue and red lights flashing and bringing Margot back to *that night*.

No. She closed her eyes. She would not allow this to take her back—not to that night. Besides, her niece was frightened and needed her to be strong.

"This is ridiculous. She's nineteen, Adam. She is *not* a killer."

His eyes reflected what she knew to be true. He and her husband had both seen terrible things in their line of work. Unfortunately, no one was too young to be capable of murder. But surely not Taylor.

She looked down at her niece and saw that she was trembling. Her fear was real enough, but she *had* lied about the man in the car. Margot had seen that much in her expression. And she'd escaped from the bathroom at the senior center. And she'd had that fight with Marco.

Margot clenched her eyes for a moment, trying to drown out all of the things that seemed to lead to Taylor's guilt. She was innocent until proven guilty—though that wouldn't happen because she *hadn't* done this awful thing.

"It's okay, honey. You go with them and do what they say. I'll call your mom and we'll figure this out."

"No!" Taylor's reply was so sharp that Adam turned to look at her from where he was briefing an officer. "I mean...can you please wait—just a day or something—to tell Renee. This will literally kill our relationship or... whatever it is. Please, Aunt Margot, don't call her. Not tonight at least."

It went against everything in Margot's makeup as a sister to agree. "I...I can't do that."

"I'm an adult," Taylor said, drilling her gaze into Margot. "Just...give me a day to figure this out."

Margot bit her lip and looked between the young girl and Adam, who now stood nearby. He was waiting to take Taylor.

"Please—promise me, Aunt Margot." Now Taylor was crying, real tears that burned trails down her cheeks. It was the first thing she'd actually gotten worked up about.

"All right," Margot heard the words come from her mouth but she hardly believed she'd said them.

"Th-thank you," Taylor said as Adam reached out toward her.

"You have the right to remain silent..."

Margot watched as if she were part of a bad dream while her niece was placed in the squad car and the door closed.

Her empty eyes stared back at Margot, Taylor's complexion as white as whipped cream. The car drove away and Margot promised herself that she would do whatever it took to clear Taylor's name because, if she knew one thing, it was the fact that Taylor had not killed Marco Rossario.

What she didn't know was why her niece's fingerprints were on the murder weapon. Or how the police knew the fingerprints were Taylor's.

CHAPTER 6

*M*argot tried her best to focus on the task at hand, but it was nearly impossible. Watching the squad car holding her niece drive away had felt like a band of iron slowly cinching around her heart. Tighter and tighter until she wasn't sure she could feel, let alone breathe, anymore.

She'd wobbled on her feet but Adam had been there, wrapping his arm securely around her shoulder and directing her onto the sidewalk next to her car so she could calm down. He wouldn't even let her get in the car, let alone think about driving, until he was sure she was somewhat settled.

Then she'd snatched the keys from his grasp and leveled her gaze at him. Even in the dim light she knew he saw every emotion written in her eyes. He was a lot like Julian in that way. She told him in no uncertain terms he *was* coming to see her and they were going to have a conversation.

But now, as she glanced at the clock and then the door for the millionth time in the span of an hour, she wasn't sure he'd agreed so much as said whatever it would take for her to let go of his arm in the vice like grip she'd had it in.

It was nearing seven o'clock—still early, but she knew Adam was on a case and that meant little sleep and lots to deal with.

Her heart sank at the thought of Taylor in a jail cell, cold and alone. She had wanted to see her immediately, but she knew she had to bake in the morning if Rosie was going to have anything to sell when she took over later that day.

Margot glanced up again, but this time her gaze collided with Adam's. He stood on the sidewalk in front of the glass-fronted door, hands lazily in his pockets. But she wasn't fooled. Inside, Adam was like a highly-strung dog ready to attack the next lead he got or any new information in the case.

She wiped the flour dust from her fingers and unlocked the front door. He held her gaze for a moment, his eyes whispering an apology for arresting her niece, but she turned her back on him. She wasn't mad at him exactly, but she knew he was wrong.

"Coffee?"

"Please."

She poured him a cup of strong Ethiopian coffee and refilled her half-empty mug as well. Handing it over, she pushed a plate of *Oopses* in front of him. They were what she called any baked goods that didn't meet her satisfaction of looking professional. She often boxed them up and either took them to the senior center or down the street to her friend Tamera's shop.

"This is the best mistake I've tasted," he said, savoring the end of a caramel pecan cinnamon roll.

She couldn't help the half-smile that slipped into place, but even that felt like a betrayal.

He's not your enemy, Marg, she reminded herself.

"Adam—" she began but he held up a hand, his eyes still closed as he popped in the last bite and then followed it up with a swig of coffee.

"Perfection." He let out a contented sigh then opened his eyes. "Okay, now we can get down to business."

She crossed her arms looking up at him. "My nineteen-year-old niece is in custody for a *murder*. One she didn't commit, by the way. I'd hardy call that business."

"I'm sorry, poor choice of words." He grimaced. "I just mean that you're full steam ahead and I haven't even finished my coffee yet," he said, holding up the cup as if it were the proof she needed.

"But Taylor—"

"Is innocent until proven guilty."

"Which is something *you* will be trying to do!" She felt her cheeks heat.

"Hold on there." A deep V appeared in the middle of his forehead. "I don't *want* Taylor to be the murderer. Don't make it sound as if I'll be finding ways to pin this on her." He huffed out a breath. "I will do everything in my power to prove her innocent if that's true. But I won't ignore facts. You know me better than that."

The look of hurt in Adam's hazel eyes pierced her conscience and she dropped her arms. "I'm sorry. You're right. I do know you better than that." It was the truth and she felt foolish for doubting him in first place. Of course he would want to see Taylor proved innocent—if she were. Margot shivered, not able to believe her niece was capable of murder.

"What do you know?" she asked tentatively.

He sighed and took another sip of coffee first. "There isn't much yet. Forensics only linked the fingerprint to Taylor, but—" He paused as if considering how much he could tell her. In all reality, he had probably told her too much already—maybe even being here was too much—but she was thankful he had come anyway. "We haven't found any other evidence linking her to the crime scene."

Margo frowned, picking at a piece of deformed macaroon. "Why, Adam?" She met his gaze and knew he understood she wasn't asking about the evidence at the crime scene.

"We've tossed out ideas like crime of passion, something stemming from the moment of their altercation at Antonio's, but there's nothing solid yet."

"Not to mention the fact she was in *my house* when this crime was supposed to have been committed."

"Right," he said, sounding unconvinced.

"But...what? What aren't you saying?"

"Obviously, from her stunt last night, she is adept at climbing out of windows. I—" He hesitated, looking down. "—checked out the window from her room. Since your house is up against the hillside, it wouldn't have been hard for her to slip out unnoticed while you slept."

The sickening feeling in her stomach was back. She knew that what he said was true. But still...

"Why? Everything you've told me seems extremely weak when we're talking about *murder*. What motive did anyone have for killing Marco Rossario?"

"We don't know enough about him yet, but believe me, we're working on it." He shifted his position slightly closer to her, looking down with intensity. "Look, I'm doing everything I can—my whole team is. You know it better than most—it takes time and hard work. I'll give it my all, I promise you that."

Warmth spread through her at his words, but it wasn't enough to chase away the chill that was slowly taking over her heart. It was going to be a long process and a messy one for Taylor, and Margot had a feeling that more skeletons would come to light before this whole thing was over.

～

Rosie burst into the kitchen, her robin's egg blue apron tied snugly around her large hips. "Honey, you best be headed out if you're going to make it in to see Taylor."

Margot knew the woman was right and she wanted to go, but her mind was lost in thoughts of their own. She couldn't stop thinking about her conversation with Adam last night.

No evidence of Taylor's presence was found at the crime scene—Miller's Bridge—but her fingerprints were on the murder weapon. That seemed like a very thin case, then again, fingerprints were a rock solid piece of evidence, weren't they? Where had the knife come from? What type was it? If Margot knew, it could help her discover some way the girl's prints had gotten on the knife other than during the murder of that poor, albeit misguided, boy.

"Hello to Mrs. Durand," Rosie said, waiving a hand in front of her face.

Margot blinked back to the present to see Rosie's smile,

her white teeth shimmering against her creamy chocolate skin.

"Well, *there* you are. Happy to have you back. Now go." She put her hands on her hips and gave a look that would have halted the Terminator.

"All right, okay, I'm going," Margot said. "Just let me finish this."

Rosie eyed the counter and nodded once. "I'm only letting you finish those because I intend to eat one—maybe more —and it would be a shame for them to sit there unfinished. But then you go." The woman bustled back to the front and she heard her loud greeting, "Welcome to the *bakery*, folks! Ready to taste the best French pastries this side of the Atlantic?"

Margot chuckled to herself, unsure where Rosie came up with half the things she said, but loving her all the more for them.

She turned her attention back to the task at hand as she whipped up the pastry cream to fill the last batch of éclair's. Her mind snagged on the evidence again. Miller's Bridge wasn't far from her shop. It was a short walk down the river walk pathway. Maybe...

She could envision the bridge, but for some reason she felt the need to *see* it in person. Maybe it would help her clear thoughts from her head. Maybe it would put more in. She wasn't sure. Either way, she felt the need to go.

Finishing off the pastries, she said good-bye to Rosie and pulled the small handmade satchel her friend Tamera had crafted onto her shoulder. She let herself out of the back door and walked down the stone pathway toward the bridge. If she timed it right, she could walk past there, get to her car, and make it to the courthouse in time for Taylor's bail hearing.

The back of her bakery looked out over the Potomac River, as did all of the shops along this stretch of riverfront property. They were situated high up on an old stonework wall lined with wrought iron fencing that added to the charm. She passed the small café situated next to her shop. The bright yellow umbrellas that covered the outdoor seating in the back mimicked the sun even if wasn't quite warm enough to be outside yet.

Then she passed the antique store that housed more than its fair share of Civil War history and paraphernalia. Then the pet shop, shoe store, and paper goods shop where she often bought her packaging materials for the bakery. At the end of the row was Tamera's craft boutique. Margot smiled, thinking of her friend on her honeymoon right now in Hawaii. She had met and married the man of her dreams at age fifty-two, giving all women hope that maybe good things did come to those who waited.

Once Margot was past the last shop, she took the pathway that diverged to the right and stayed level with the river. The breeze was stiff and the river looked more choppy than normal, but the sun helped balance out the cold.

A few more minutes of walking and she turned the bend to see Miller's Bridge above her. It stretched out across the river and was tinged with a green patina and looked more industrial than anything else. It was functional, but not for cars—not anymore. Now only foot traffic, bikes, and the occasional mother with a stroller used it to cross over to the small island in the middle of the Potomac. The bridge had once continued across the river to another peninsula that looped back up into northern Virginia, but that bridge had long since been taken down and now only this small portion of it remained.

Yellow police tape snapped in the wind, closing off the path for everyone and screaming that something bad had happened here. From her low vantage point she could see that no one was at the scene, then again, she hadn't really expected the police to *still* be there, had she?

She looked across the railing sections, but nothing appeared out of the ordinary. Looking down and out across the river, some of the rocks were visible above the waterline. She knew many more lay just beneath the surface as well. To someone living, they would have been perilous.

Margot shivered at the thought, reaching up to wrap her arms around herself to ward off the chill, but it went deeper.

Seeing all that she could from the path, she took the steps that led up to the bridge's entrance from street level. The bright yellow tape warned her to stay off of the bridge and she obeyed it, but she could still see well enough to the middle of the bridge from her vantage point.

The railing was tall, at least waist-height if not slightly taller, depending on a person's height. She envisioned Marco from the night before, trying her best to distance herself from what had happened. She assumed the railing would have hit him in the middle of the back.

She used her phone to snap pictures of the bridge from several angles for later observation and checked her watch. It was time to get to the courthouse.

Reaching the tall building, she ran up the steps and made it through the meager security with plenty of time to spare. As she sat in the courtroom and her clock ticked five minutes past the hearing time, she frowned. She was in the right room, wasn't she?

Then a thin clerk with mousey brown hair and a low and tight bun stepped onto the floor. "The bail hearing of Miss Taylor Garvey will be postponed until tomorrow afternoon."

Margot felt her pulse spike. Postponed? Why? What was going on?

She picked up her satchel and rushed out of the large double doors and straight into Adam's solid chest. He reached out and steadied her. "There you are."

"Why is it postponed?"

He blinked, catching up quickly. "Judge Castor is sick and

Judge Pellenworth couldn't spare time for another case. It's been a madhouse."

"So my niece has to stay another day in *jail* because someone is sick? This is ridiculous." Margot heard the desperation and anger in her tone, even felt the gazes from many in the echoing atrium where they stood, but she didn't care. This was Taylor they were talking about. What happened to 'innocent until proven guilty'?

"Come on," he said, as if sensing her meltdown. "I'll get you in to see her."

CHAPTER 7

*M*argot felt the chill enter her the minute she stepped into the jailhouse. She hated knowing that her niece was staying there and she hated the fact that she hadn't told her sister yet.

Adam helped her sign in and then she walked down the hallway toward the holding cell. Taylor looked small, dwarfed by the orange coveralls she wore. She sat on the bed, knees to her chest and looking forlorn. It tugged at Margot's heart and she felt like a failure.

How had she allowed her niece to be arrested for murder? Julian would have done something—could have...what? Foreseen that this would happen? No. As good of a detective as Julian was, there was no way he could have prevented this. Maybe she shouldn't have agreed for the girl to come out to visit. Then again, did Marco's death have something to do with her niece or was it a case of mistaken identity or being in the wrong place at the wrong time?

Those excuses both felt flimsy even as she thought them. Fingerprints on a murder weapon didn't just happen. They were either left by the killer or planted there.

That thought churned her stomach even more. Was her niece being framed for the murder of some part-time waiter? Or had she really been involved?

"Aunt Marg," Taylor said, standing up so fast she nearly fell over.

She rushed to the bars and Margot could see tears in her eyes, which made her appear even younger. No, this little girl didn't have any hand in murder. She may be nineteen, but she was innocent. Margot felt it in her gut— something her husband had said was a good indicator.

Adam had remained at the entrance, promising to wait for her while she spoke with Taylor, but now she wanted to simply sit on the floor and wait with her niece. It wasn't possible, of course, but it felt so wrong knowing that she would have to leave the girl behind.

"They canceled your bail hearing for today," she found herself saying.

"I know." She dropped her gaze, her slim fingers gripping the bars. "Someone came in and told me. I—I guess I have to wait until tomorrow."

"I'm sorry, sweetie," she said, wishing she could wrap her

up in a hug. "I'll be there at the hearing tomorrow. I'll post bail and we'll get you out of there, all right?"

She nodded, tears filling her eyes again. "No matter what they said—" Her voice broke. "I didn't do it."

"I know, Tay. I know you wouldn't do anything like that."

She dropped her gaze, her knuckles turning white on the bars. "I wouldn't kill anyone."

"I need to call your mother—"

"Please," she interrupted. "Please don't call her. Not yet. I...I want to be the one to tell her. I'll be out on bail tomorrow, right? I can call her then."

Margot felt like she was betraying her sister, but Taylor was also an adult and she couldn't force her. Then again...

"If you don't call her tomorrow, I will."

Taylor met her gaze for a moment then finally nodded. "Okay."

"Ma'am," an officer said, coming down the hall, "I'm afraid that's all the time you have."

She nodded then looked back at Taylor. "Stay strong, sweetie. I'm going to find out who did this."

Taylor looked shocked by her words, but Margot didn't take them back or provide any explanation. She just knew that she would do anything to help this wide-eyed young girl whom her husband had written letters to. This young woman who had her life ahead of her.

Forcing her own tears back, Margot squeezed Taylor's fingers through the bars then turned to be escorted out. Her heart ached at leaving her niece there, but she knew she could do far more good tracking down who had framed her niece for Marco's murder, because at this point, that was the only plausible reality.

"CAN I TAKE YOU TO LUNCH?" Adam asked when they were back outside and she could feel the freedom to breathe again. The air of the jail had been stifling.

She considered the fact that she was hungry, but also the reality that she needed time—and distance—to think about her next move.

"Not today. I'm sorry, Adam," she said, shrugging. "Another time?"

"Of course. Sorry—bad timing."

"I'll see you later."

He looked at her through narrowed lashes, the dark fringe making his hazel eyes appear mysterious. "You're not going to do anything...foolish, are you?"

"What do you mean?" Her eyebrows rose in surprise.

He considered her, his hands casually resting in the

pockets of his light gray slacks. "I know you, Margot. Julian talked to me about you and he said that, on more than one occasion, you got in over your head in following along with his cases."

She feigned ignorance. "I don't know what you're talking about."

"Ah, but you do," he said, pointing a finger at her. "See— that look right there. It tells me that you know *exactly* what I'm talking about."

She stared him down. If he wanted her to say she wouldn't try and clear her niece's name, then *he* was the foolish one. But she wouldn't give him the satisfaction of thinking he'd pegged her.

"Just...be careful." The pleading in his tone surprised her, but she tried not to let it show.

"I'm a baker, Adam. How dangerous can that be?"

He shook his head, a small smile slipping onto his handsome features. "Right."

She headed for her car, her mind scattering to a million different things. Where she should go next. Adam's warning. The look on Taylor's face. Adam's invitation to lunch—

Her stomach grumbled. Lunch wasn't a bad idea. Turning the car on, she contemplated where she should go to grab a quiet bite. Her gaze trailed the distance then dropped in front of her. The receipt in the middle console caught her attention.

Antonio's.

"Of course!" she said to the empty car.

It was a short and familiar drive to *Pane Dolce* and, before she could think past what she would say to her favorite Italian restaurant owner on the death of one of his employees, she was asking for the secluded corner booth and to see Antonio when he had a spare moment.

The large, usually jovial man joined her at the table, sliding in across from her with a heavy sigh.

"*Mia bella,* what is this world coming to? Eh?"

She offered him a sad smile. "I'm sorry about Marco."

"*Pfft,*" he said, waving a hand at her. "I am as shocked as you are—and dare I say, as unaffected." He looked apologetic. "I mean, I feel bad for the boy…to go in such a way." He made a face of disgust. "But some would say he had it coming to him."

"What do you mean?" she said, trying not to sound too interested.

"He was a—how do they say? *Playboy.* I hired him, as I told you, because of Lorenzo, but if I hadn't let him go that night you were here, I would have let him go soon. He wasn't a good worker. Flirting with all the women. And he was late. *Whew,* late all the time because of his 'errands'." He made a motion of air quotes and gave her a knowing look.

"Errands?" she repeated. "What do you mean?"

The man shrugged, motioning a waiter over. "Margot Durand, meet my nephew Lorenzo."

She looked up at the dark-haired boy with tan skin and striking blue eyes. He was handsome in a model-looking type way, but he looked less sure of himself. Unlike Marco, he barely made eye contact with her, only muttering an obligatory greeting.

Antonio ordered for her without even asking, telling his nephew to put a rush on it, then turned to look back at her.

"I am not sure of these errands..." He arched his eyebrows at her. "But the car he drove and the clothes he wore on his days off—you know, when he'd come in to pick up his check—they were fancy. Too fancy for what I was giving him."

Margot nodded, trying to piece things together in her head. A rich, playboy-type who ran suspicious errands on the side.

"Drugs?" she asked.

"No!" Antonio shook his head violently. "None of my employees use drugs. I do the tests and make it all legal."

She smiled to assuage him, but in the back of her mind

she was thinking of all of the ways Marco could have passed the test without actually being drug-free. Then again, Antonio would have noticed in his behavior if he'd been a user. Maybe a dealer then? But why have the job at Antonio's?

"There you are," came a syrupy voice attached to a lithe figure clad in impossibly tight workout clothes. "Antonio, you simply *must* agree to cater my party. I won't take no for an answer. Oh, hello, Margot."

Margot looked up to see Mrs. Penberthy. Her fake smile matched her clothing choices—plastered on.

"Oh, Kim, nice to see you," Margot said through a forced smile of her own.

"But really, Antonio..." She paused to type something out on the cell phone that was permanently attached to her hand. "I need to hear a yes out of you. Just one simple word. Come on now. You know I get what I want." She leaned forward and placed a finger on the side of Antonio's round face, tapping to accentuate each word. "Just. One. Word."

Margot resisted the urge to roll her eyes. Kim Penberthy was over-the-top in every sense of the phrase. Maybe it was something that worked well for her station as wife to the mayor, but in small company—or really *any* company—it was too much in Margot's opinion.

"Ah, my dear Mrs. Penberthy. You flatter me," Antonio said, eating up the attention. "You have persuaded me. I shall be happy to cater your party. My assistant will set everything up for you. I shall do my famous lasagna, no?"

"Uh, no," she said, wrinkling her nose. "I love it, don't get me wrong, Tony, but this needs to be...stunning."

"Stunning?" he repeated, looking confused.

"I'll do some research and get back to you. It'll be a party like no one has seen before. Ta ta," she said, tossing a hand over her shoulder as her long blonde ponytail swished about her shoulders.

"Stunning?" Antonio said, looking back at Margot. "Is my lasagna not stunning?"

Fighting back a smile, Margot reassured him with a pat on the hand. "It is."

Her lunch arrived and Antonio stood, wishing her a good day and a happy lunch—on him. She shook her head but he insisted before chasing after a waiter who was apparently taking a plate to a table without the proper garnish.

Margot ate the pasta dish while her thoughts centered on Marco. He had money. He was often late. He ran errands. It didn't mean anything other than the fact that there was much more to Marco Rossario than she had first expected. And that information could hold the key to his murder.

CHAPTER 8

*M*argot checked her text messages as she walked back to her car, the memory of the brief encounter with Marco and Taylor that night coming back to her and momentarily distracting her. Something about it felt off—why had he risked coming outside to see Taylor? Obviously, he was either very much besotted with her niece or…there was something else behind it. What had he said? Something about wanting something?

Slipping into the sun-warmed car, Margot felt the affects of her less than restful night's sleep. Her brain felt foggy, her memory compromised. How was she supposed to rest comfortably knowing that Taylor was in a jail cell?

She stifled a yawn and looked down when her phone vibrated in her hand. It was a message from Bentley asking her to come to the senior center. After a quick call to Rosie to make sure everything was running smoothly at the bakery, she put the car in gear and drove to the dilapidated building.

She found a parking spot near the lot and jogged up the steps to the center's entrance. Gone were the few decorations that had been put up for the World Dinner Night. The main area of the center looked as drab and worn down as she felt from lack of sleep, but she pushed past it and headed for the perpetually filled coffee pot.

Fortified with liquid energy, she headed to Bentley's favorite spot. There was a small reading nook located at the back of the building. Since the center was situated on the side of a hill—like most of the town—the view was spectacular. It looked out over the town and to the river. On clear days like today, you could see boats and all manner of seagulls dotting the horizon.

"There you are," he said, putting down the large novel he was reading. Probably something by Grisham, she thought. Bentley seemed to worship the guy.

"Hey, Bentley," she said, leaning to kiss his cheek. "Got your text. What's going on?"

He shifted over and she joined him on the window seat. "I've got a bad feeling."

"Is this about what you were telling me last night? I really don't think—"

"Oh, you poor dear." Margot and Bentley turned to see Lynellen standing there, hands clasped together in front of her bosom, eyes almost teary. "I heard what happened. You must be beside yourself, you poor dear."

Without warning, Lynellen came toward Margot with outstretched arms and suddenly Margot was encased by the scent of baby powder and a cheap knock off of Chanel No. 5.

"I—I'm," Margot coughed. "Wait, what are you talking about?"

Lynellen shook her head, the sheen of tears unmistakable at this close distance. "That poor, sweet, innocent—or not —" She glanced to the side with a worried look. "—niece of yours. Struck down in her youth."

"She's not dead, Lynellen," Bentley was quick to correct her.

"No, but she might as well be for the world of trouble she's in." Lynellen shook her head. "I'm so sorry to hear about all of the problems our youth get in these days. Just the other day, I was telling my grandson that—"

"Lynellen," Bentley interrupted, "I know it's tragic and all, but I'm having a chat with Margot here."

"Oh. Yes." Lynellen nodded emphatically, "Smart, consulting a lawyer and all. Though don't you think you should get one who still practices?"

Margot shot Bentley a surprised look but he was too busy convincing Lynellen to leave them alone. When she'd finally wandered off Margot folded her arms and met Bentley's gaze.

"You were a lawyer?"

He shrugged. "I did my time as a defense attorney back in the old days. But that's not why I have you here. Though it is a shame to hear about Taylor. I don't believe it for a second. And know that I wouldn't be bothering you at such a time, but...I've just got this feeling."

Margot took a moment to take in an image of Bentley in a suit arguing at trials—it explained the Grisham obsession. She blinked. Right. She needed to finish up this conversation and then move on to her next step in helping Taylor, even though she wasn't sure what that step should be.

"What is it?"

His furrowed brow deepened. "It's about what I told you last night. Someone is stealing money from our fundraisers. I've thought about going to the police, but all of the papers we have *show* that my gut is wrong...but I feel it, here." He tapped the middle of his chest. "Something is off."

Margot blinked. Could this in some way be connected with Marco's murder? It was a stretch—no, it wasn't even that. It was pure conjecture and guesswork, something Julian had told her never to do, but she couldn't ignore the timing of it all. Could she?

"Margot?"

"Sorry. I was lost in the land of *what if.*"

"Well, come back to the present," he said gruffly. Bentley was more ornery than usual. "I'm sorry," he said, shaking his head, "I just can't believe that anyone would have the gall to pull a stunt like this. We just want our lodge—what's so bad about that? But everyone else on the committee swears things are in order." He tossed up his hands. "It's like I'm talking to a bunch of sheep, I tell you. You'd have to be a heartless fool to target senior citizens, wouldn't you?"

It was a valid question. Was someone stealing money to benefit themselves or was it actually a roadblock to the lodge's construction?

"I don't know, Bentley. It does seem like a cowardly thing to do." *If it's happening.* She hated the hint of suspicion in her thoughts.

"I need you to do something for me."

Margot felt wariness creep up on her. She was someone who often had trouble saying no—to anything—and the look in Bentley's eyes told her she wouldn't be able to turn him down either.

"What?" she said, letting out a sigh.

"I need you to go to the mayor's office tomorrow to see if you can talk to Eve, the mayor's assistant. I can't be sure, but I think she knows something about all this."

"What do you expect me to do?" Margot said, laughing. "Barge in there and give her the inquisition?"

"I've got a theory." Bentley leaned in closer, whispering conspiratorially, "I want you to tell her that you're interested in doing a fundraiser to, I don't know, add on to your bakery or something, and see how she responds."

Margot was already shaking her head. "Bentley, that is ridiculous. One, I have no space to expand and everyone knows that, and two, what do you think she'll do? Open up and tell me she's got a great way to make money— stealing from senior citizens?"

"No. Not at all. See, that's the beauty of it. She'll just *know* about the scheme and we'll see what goes on from there. Word has it *she* was the one who recommended the kid who does our finances."

Margot fought to keep up. "Wait, you think Eve is in on this?"

Bentley leaned back, his frown deepening. "I think she might be."

Margot nearly laughed. "Eve is one of the sweetest people I know."

"Margot," Bentley said admonishingly. "Julian taught you better than that. She may *look* innocent, but that doesn't mean she is."

Margot had a hard time seeing the former school teacher turned stay-at-home-mom turned assistant to the mayor as anything but sweet. Still, it was odd that she had recommended someone who had turned out not to be 'above board.' *If Bentley's right.* There it was again—that hint of doubt.

"I still don't see it, but I'll reserve judgment."

"Good girl."

"Okay, one more question." She stared Bentley down. "Who is this mysterious accountant?"

"I don't know really, had good credentials—or so I thought. Name's Lorenzo something."

Margot sucked in a breath. *Lorenzo?!*

"Lorenzo Bianchi?"

"Yeah, that's the kid. Wait—he's not doing any accounting for you, is he?"

"No," she said, her gaze trailing out over the window and to the water beyond. He wasn't, but he was definitely now on her radar.

MARGOT HAD STAYED up too late. It was nearly impossible for her to fall asleep at eight like she usually did. Her mind had whirred a hundred miles a minute with worry about Taylor, thoughts about Marco chased by the image of Lorenzo Bianchi, and the curiosity of how this all fit together—if it did. Somehow.

Again, Julian's voice came back to her

Sometimes, ma chérie, it is not the obvious that draws two things together but the lack of an obvious connection that does it.

An ache had filled her chest with a longing to talk all of this over with Julian. She'd almost called Adam, but it wasn't a good idea. Knowing him and knowing that he was part of this case—a vital part—she couldn't risk him knowing of her involvement in anything until she had solid evidence. If then.

When sleep had finally found her, it had been restless and lacking.

Now, she was in the midst of her morning routine with an added batch of croissants for her trip to the mayor's office later that day. It felt dishonest to be planning this trip with the express intent of gaining information on a woman she respected, let alone liked and went to church with, but how could she dismiss the fact that Eve had recommended Lorenzo?

Still, the facts weren't lining up. If Eve was somehow part of this scheme—something Margot wasn't convinced of— then why had she asked for help with a car bill from their women's group?

Unless…Margot stiffened, standing up and forcing her shoulders to relax. No, Eve couldn't have slipped into something illegal because of money problems. Then

again, money was the root of most evils in this world—
not to mention a great motive.

Margot thought of what motive there had been for
Marco's death. Maybe she would talk to Adam again, but
only to find out if he had any leads on that aspect...if he'd
tell her. That still remained to be seen.

The pastries in the oven to bake, she cleaned up around
the shop, took note of what items she needed to restock,
and then made a quick reminder to contact Adam after
the bail hearing. Just the thought of it made her sick to
her stomach. She needed to contact her sister and—

A thought struck Margot. Taylor was usually texting on
her phone twenty-four/seven. She assumed that she
texted her mother some of that time. Then again, did
nineteen-year olds still text their parents? Would Renee
worry?

But Margot pushed the thought from her mind. Her sister
had *her* number. She could always call her, couldn't she?

Feeling flustered and over-tired, Margot sunk down into
her desk chair and, setting an alarm for seven, rested her
head back against the cushioned headrest.

BEEPING and pounding wove together to create a strange
sort of dream for Margot. She was in a burning building
about to jump from the third story into the arms of a

waiting fireman, though how she would make it she had no idea. The beeping of the fire truck backing up reminded her if she waited, she could just climb down the ladder but the pounding of the fire behind her was too fast, too loud, she would have to jump and—

She gasped and sat upright, the alarm on her phone sounding and the pounding from her dream a reality. She rushed to the front door, relieved to see Bentley there, morning paper under his arm.

He grinned, nodding in the direction of her hair. "Sleeping on the job, I see."

"I didn't sleep well last night." She reached up and felt the bump of her hair. "The usual."

"Yep. And tell me you're planning on making a trip—"

"To the mayor's office, yes," she said, grinning. "Give me one minute to get your order."

The rest of the morning went by quickly and when Rosie came to take over for the afternoon, she had her box of croissants—some even chocolate-filled, the mayor's favorite—ready to go. With a wave goodbye, she headed out the door.

She pulled into a space across the street from the office and took a deep breath, staying in the car. She wasn't exactly sure how to play this. She remembered Julian's comments about his undercover work in his younger years, but that had mostly been gang related. She shivered just thinking about her late husband keeping company with gang members.

Movement across the street drew her attention. The mayor, potbelly stomach leading the way, stepped from the office and donned his fedora. His gaze trailed around, a look of pride settling over his features. She smiled. Though she didn't agree with him on all of his political platforms, he was a nice man. She was about to race out to catch him when a thought brought an invisible hand down on her shoulder.

She was really here to see Eve. Wasn't this better?

She let the mayor get into his car and drive away before she stepped out into the warm sunshine and darted across the street. The small electronic beep indicated her entrance into the office and she went down the hallway to where Eve's desk sat.

The woman looked up, a smile creasing her face. She pulled her glasses off and rested her elbows on the desk in front of her.

"Margot Durand, this is a surprise. Are those for me?" she said with a conspiratorial laugh.

"Afraid not. I thought I'd drop these off for the mayor. Croissants, his favorite."

"He's going to love that—though Kim would have a fit if she knew." Eve's eyes drew wide. "You can leave them with me. I won't eat more than one, I promise." She winked.

"Oh sure—and you really should have one! There are more than enough for the mayor."

Eve accepted the yellow box and placed it under the high counter of her desk. Then she looked back up at Margot, probably wondering what she was still doing there.

"I, uh..." This was the part Margot wasn't good with. Fabrication. "I'm considering doing a fundraiser. You know, new bakery equipment isn't cheap. I'd heard someone mention you knew a good accountant?" She held her breath. Everything she'd said wasn't a complete lie. She *had* considered doing a fundraiser and bakery equipment *was* expensive.

"Actually, I do." Eve leaned forward. "But I have to preface this with the fact that he's not a real accountant —well, yet."

This wasn't what Margot had expected. "Um, what do you mean?"

"I'm doing night school—remember I mentioned it at our women's Bible study at the beginning of the year. Anyway, I've met some amazing people there—all trying to get their lives on track or start a new business. Things like that. And this young man is exceptional. I overheard our teacher talking about him and said he was his best student. I've referred him to a few people."

So that was why Eve had recommended Lorenzo to the senior center. "Wow. Sounds great. Can I get his contact information?"

"Sure!" She beamed as she wrote it out on a sticky note. "Here you go."

"Thanks. I really appreciate this." Then, turning to go, she said, "Enjoy that croissant."

"Oh, you know I will."

CHAPTER 9

*T*he bail hearing went faster than Margot had expected and soon she was in the hallway waiting for Taylor to get changed. She saw Adam from across the room, but officers surrounded him and it looked like he was in a heated conversation. No matter, she had nothing to talk with him about anyway. Not yet at least.

Though she did have a call to make to the night school teacher. The thought of Lorenzo being a bright, shining star in accounting would surely explain a lot for his skills with hiding money from the senior center—if that was what was happening.

She pulled out her phone and ran a quick search for the local night school. It wasn't difficult to find the teacher who dealt with most of the math classes. Thankfully, his phone number was listed and, with a glance around to make sure Taylor wasn't coming yet, she made the call.

It rang four times then slipped to voicemail. Uncertain of what to say, she merely said she was looking for information regarding one of his classes. Leaving her information, she pressed end and turned to see Taylor walking down the hall in the clothes Margot had brought for her.

"Hey, sweetie," she said, wrapping her arms around the girl. "How you doing?"

"Can we just go home?"

"Of course." She maneuvered them out of the courthouse and soon they were on the way home. Taylor nearly raced up the steps, but she didn't blame the girl.

Once they were inside, she turned to look at Taylor, arms crossed. "We need to call your mom."

"I know." Her shoulders slumped.

"Why don't I make us coffee and you can call her." Handing Taylor her phone, Margot turned to the coffeemaker and began to prepare a pot with fresh, dark grounds.

She tried not to overhear what her niece was saying, but it was nearly impossible. Things weren't going well. Then, with stomping feet and an explosion of air from clenched teeth, Taylor came back into the kitchen and thrust the phone at her.

"She wants to talk to you."

An uneasy feeling twisting in the pit of her stomach, she accepted the phone. "Hey, Rae."

"My daughter was charged with murder and you didn't even think to call me! And I trusted you to take care of her and keep her out of trouble! I'm getting on the next flight! I'll be there as soon as I can."

Margot took a deep breath and nodded for Taylor to help herself to the coffee while she walked into the living room, sinking onto the bright white couch that nestled in golden light coming in from the windows.

As she explained what had happened, her sister attempted to interrupt almost every sentence but she finally got to the end. "I know we should have called, but it was Taylor's choice and I honored that."

The silence on the other end of the line was telling. "What will Dillon think?" Her sister's voice was small, almost too quiet to hear.

"It's going to be okay. She didn't do this and the police will find that out."

"She's got a record." Renee almost whimpered. "It's sealed, but with a murder case, they'll dig. I just know it."

Margot cringed, but didn't let that enter her voice. At least that explained how the police had Taylor's fingerprints on file. "She didn't do this, Rae. She's innocent and the law will prove that." *I'll prove that.*

Finally, after half an hour, Renee finally agreed not to fly out. She only relented after Margot reminded her that there was nothing she could do—yet. They would wait it out and see what was going on. When they knew more, then she'd come.

"That was pretty bad," Taylor said, slumping onto the couch.

Margot shook her head. "Do you know Lorenzo Bianchi?"

Was it her imagination or did Taylor pale?

"No. Who's that?"

Was her niece lying to her?

"He's—" A knock on the door interrupted her explanation and she opened it to find Adam, Chinese carryout in both hands and a smile on his face.

"Thought you ladies might like some lunch."

She smiled, glancing back to Taylor. Her niece looked at Adam warily, no doubt wondering at first if he'd been there to take her back to captivity.

"Come on in."

He did and, as soon as the food was opened, Taylor took her plate to her room and shut the door.

"How are you doing?" Adam asked, using chopsticks to pick out a piece of broccoli.

Margot massaged her temples. "I've been better."

"And Taylor?"

"I don't know." She looked up at Adam. "Have you learned anything more?"

His gaze narrowed. "You're not asking me to share information of an active case are you?"

She allowed a weary smile to answer him.

"The only thing I can say at this point is that I'm struggling to find a connection between Taylor and Marco. No texts, calls, nothing. It's… It doesn't make any sense. As much as I'd initially thought the crime was one of passion, the facts aren't adding up."

So it was premeditated?

"Why would my niece—who knows no one here in town —murder some random man in a premeditated manner? Come on, Adam. This doesn't make any sense"

"And yet her fingerprints were on the knife from Ant—" He slammed his mouth shut.

Antonio's. Of course!

"Look, forget I said anything. Just keep her out of trouble and if you hear anything, you come to me. You hear me, Margot?"

"Sure, if I—" Her phone rang and she checked the caller

ID. She recognized the number of the night school professor. "Sorry, I've got to take his."

He nodded and she slipped into the kitchen.

"Hello, this is Margot Durand."

"Hello, Ms. Durand, this is Frank Crestwood. I had a call from you."

"Yes, I just had a quick question regarding your accounting class." She cringed, hoping that Adam wasn't listening in. She pushed further into the kitchen.

"Oh, are you interested in a class? We have one scheduled for the summer, but it doesn't start for a few more weeks."

"Um, no, actually. I was interested in knowing who your best student is."

He hesitated. "My best...student?"

"Yes, my friend Eve is in that class and she'd mentioned the name of your best student. I have a project I need a little accounting help on, nothing major of course, and I thought it would be nice to give someone a chance while they're still in school. I own the *Parisian Pâtisserie*."

"Oh, I see. Well, in that case hands down it's Victor Karvo. Great guy. Very promising."

"Not Lorenzo Bianchi?"

"Lorenzo—" The man broke into a fit of laugher. "I'm sorry.

That was unprofessional." Margot rolled her eyes. "He's... trying his best. But I wouldn't lump him in with the best. Would you like me to give you Victor's contact information?"

Rather than raise suspicion, she accepted the information and hung up. So either Eve was in on the scheme and recommending Lorenzo had been part of the whole conspiracy...or, what was more likely, is that she over heard Frank talking about his best student and gotten the wrong name.

If Lorenzo wasn't doing well in class then why had he agreed to—

"Did I hear you say Lorenzo Bianchi?"

Margo froze, her stomach clenching.

"Eavesdropping?" she said, spinning around. "Would you like some coffee?"

"Don't change the subject, Margot. What was that call about?"

She merely smiled. "Coffee?"

He crossed his arms over his chest, the taut fabric of his light blue button-down stretching. "Don't do this, Margot."

"I'm not *doing* anything other than offering you coffee." She smiled sweetly but saw the distrust behind Adam's eyes.

She knew the risks involved, but weren't they worth it if

that meant she would free her niece? No matter what she uncovered, she would turn it all over to Adam anyway—she just had to have enough *to* give him. Not hints of conjecture and speculation.

No. She would need hard facts, which meant she needed to start rocking the boat.

CHAPTER 10

The next morning found Margot delivering a stack of cookie boxes to the senior center. It was still early and she'd negotiated for Rosie and Taylor to run the shop that morning with a promise that she would be back that afternoon to take over.

Bentley made a bee-line for her the minute she stepped inside, but the rest of the senior residents who'd been caught in the midst of a ping pong tournament also swarmed her but for a different reason.

When the boxes were taken and she was left alone, Bentley all but carried her to a corner.

"Well," he said, leaning in toward her. "How did it go? What did she say? Do you think she's in on it?" His inquisitive nature made her laugh, but she could also see traces of the former prosecutor in him. How had she not known he was a lawyer before?

"I went to the mayor's office," she said, glancing around as if this were a top secret meeting in the senior center of all places. "Eve definitely has nothing to do with it."

She explained what she'd found out from her friend and the subsequent call with the professor.

"See? She recommended him for the simple fact that she'd heard—mistakenly—he was the best in the class."

"Hearsay," Bentley murmured.

"Don't you dare lawyer me." She squared her shoulders at the older man. "I know and trust Eve. You're not the only one with gut feelings."

He raised a hand as if to wave off her comment. "It's too coincidental."

"I'd go to the beginning of all of this. Who said it was a good idea to hire a kid who was in night classes anyway?"

"Kim Penberthy."

"Kim," Margot repeated, frowning. "What in the world is Kim doing with her hand in senior center politics?"

"Kim's got her hands in a lot of things." Bentley shrugged. "Speak of the devil."

Margot followed his gaze to the door where Kim Penberthy had just walked in. She gave a once-over of the room then waved to someone on the other side. When she walked past, she halted when she saw Margot.

"Fancy seeing you here." She looked between Margot and Bentley. "What's that, three times in one week?" She let out a fake laugh.

"It is a small town," Margot pointed out.

"Why are you here?" she said, narrowing her gaze and looking between them.

"Dropped off some cookies."

"Here to see me." They spoke at the same time and Kim raised her eyebrows.

"Dropped off cookies," Margot said, pointing to the nearly empty boxes on the table near the ping-pong tournament group. "Then came to talk to Bentley."

"I see." Kim's tone turned cool. Then with another fake smile, she strutted away, her four-inch heels cutting a leather-clad path through the room toward a group of the more stylish senior center visitors.

"Women's group," Bentley explained.

"Strange. I had no idea she was connected here."

"I think she golfs with Sharon at the Passaeo Club once a month. Wives of past mayors or something." Bentley turned his attention back to Margot and away from the group of women who kept shooting them strange glances. "Probably heard we were getting a committee together and wanted her hand in yet another thing in this town. As if her husband didn't try and run enough of it."

"Bentley," Margot reprimanded.

"Eh, I've never liked politics." He rolled his eyes. "But back to this Lorenzo kid—"

"I'll look into it, okay?"

Bentley's pale blue eyes met hers. "Hey, you take care of that niece of yours, all right? I'll see what I can find out about him."

She was about to disagree but with the look on his face and the reality that there wasn't enough time in the day, she nodded in agreement.

"Keep me posted."

"You betcha." He grinned, wagging his eyebrows.

Margot headed back to the bakery, mind on the cases. She snorted into the quiet interior of the car. Cases? Since when had she labeled herself a detective? Then again, that was what they were. One, a case of murder involving her niece. Two, a case of missing money supposedly stolen from the senior center building fund. Three, the case of whether or not Lorenzo was a good kid or a calculated thief. Then again, was her overly suspicious, retired lawyer friend to blame for the second and third cases? Was there even an issue there? Without seeing their books, she wasn't sure what she could do.

Walking into the shop, she heard a little yelp and, thankful that they had no customers, dashed to the back of the shop where her niece was nearly on the floor, a huge sack of flour toppled on its side. Mercifully, it was unopened, but still her heart did a little leap at the sight.

"Thank *goodness* you're back. Rosie here is no help and I'm just weak apparently."

Rosie grinned at this. "I told that youngster I ain't getting down there, risking my back going out again. Uh uh. No way, no how."

"Of course not, Rosie." Margot shook her head and donned an apron. "You really can't get this up on the counter?" She looked at Taylor skeptically.

"What?" Taylor said, shrugging. "I don't lift weights or anything."

Bending down, she helped the girl lift the flour up onto the counter. It landed with a thud and a poof of white dust.

"Whew. I'm out." Taylor dusted off her hands and removed her apron.

Margot had promised that Taylor could go home when she came back, but now worry seeped into that decision.

"Wait, you're not having second thoughts, are you?" Taylor leaned forward. "You are! I can see it in your eyes. Come on, Aunt Marg, I'm exhausted. We were here at three-thirty!"

"Late mornin' for you, eh, girl?" Rosie observed.

Margot grinned at her friend and fellow worker. She knew when Margot usually showed up.

"I'll take her home," Rosie said.

"You drive?" Taylor asked.

"Taylor!" Margot reprimanded but Rosie was already laughing.

"Better than you, girl. Come on." As she walked past, Rosie put her hand on Margot's arm. "Don't worry. The Lord's in charge. I'll see that she gets home, but He'll see that she's safe."

With her friend's reassurance, she nodded and grabbed Taylor in a hug. "Stay at my place, okay?"

"I will," she said, meeting Margot's gaze. Hopefully it was the truth.

MARGOT HAD JUST FINISHED PREPPING everything for the morning, affording her and Taylor an extra hour of sleep, when her gaze snagged on the oversized bag of flour. It had taken her *and* Taylor to lift the fifty-pound bag up onto the counter. Only fifty-pounds but that was a lot to the nineteen-year old. It would be a lot to most women.

Her mind started whirring. If she remembered what Adam had said correctly, then Marco had been stabbed at the bridge and *then* gone over the railing. The tall railing.

Was it even physically possible for Taylor to hoist a grown man, let alone one who looked like working out was more than a hobby, over the railing? It didn't seem possible.

She finished her preparations and closed the shop, exiting out the back door instead of the front this time. The day had turned from warm to chilly, clouds coming in from over the ocean just beyond the peninsula across the river. She wrapped her arms around herself as she walked down the path that led to Miller's Bridge again.

Even from the distance, when the bridge came into view, her doubts were rooted more firmly. There was no way her niece could have gotten a grown man over the railing —which would be at least chest-height to her—after stabbing him. She'd said it herself, she didn't lift weights and she couldn't have lifted him.

Then again, could adrenaline account for that extra strength? But then, wouldn't there have been blood all over Taylor? Where would she have washed it off? Where had those clothes gone? Wouldn't she have incurred bruises from her encounter with Marco on the bridge? It was unlikely she—or anyone—could have stabbed him without a fight.

She stepped over a crack in the cobble stone path, pausing to look out to the river over the low stonewall. This was a place of history but now all it reminded her of was murder. And now fear that she might not be able to prove Taylor's innocence.

Then again, it wasn't up to her, was it?

A gust of wind brushed past her just as the bushes at the side of the pathway rustled. Likely a squirrel looking for—

A dark figure rushed from the bushes toward her, covered from head to foot in dark clothing. It barreled straight into her, sending her stumbling backwards with the force. When her calves hit the low rock wall, she tipped back with a scream escaping her lungs.

Then she fell over the side.

CHAPTER 11

"*A*re you sure you're all right?" Adam said. His deep hazel eyes held such compassion, but she was angry more than anything else.

"I'm fine. Just mad at myself." Margot pushed a wet strand of hair out of her eyes.

He frowned. "What? Why?"

"How did I not see them coming? And my favorite pair of Ralph Lauren flats are gone."

Adam actually laughed at that, but sobered quickly. "I'll buy you another pair. I promise. But do you feel up to telling me what happened?"

Margot shuddered, pulling the blanket more tightly around her wet shoulders and thinking back to the terrifying moment when she'd fallen over the side of the cliff down toward the water. Thankfully, her brain jumped into action and she'd righted herself in the fall in time for the water to accept her pointed feet with a minimal splash and thankfully no rocks.

She'd been lucky, so said the man who'd heard her scream and found the river access ladder. He'd helped her up when she'd surfaced, no worse for wear aside from being cold and missing her favorite shoes.

She explained she was taking a walk—for the moment leaving out her assumptions that had led to the walk—and had suddenly been shoved over the side of the low rock wall by a fast-moving mass in black. She recounted what she could remember. Black hoody. Black knit facemask. Black track pants.

"Anything stand out to you? Logos? Skin color? Height? Build?"

She closed her eyes to walk herself through what she'd seen. "At first I'd assumed they were large, but I think the clothing was actually baggy. When they hit me, it felt more like...I don't know, something bony wrapped in softness."

She opened her eyes at Adam's chuckle. "Want to explain that one?"

"I can't. I mean... Whoever it was came at me like a freight train and carried enough steam to push me over the ledge, but they weren't exactly bulky. Just strong."

Adam took notes in his small notebook. "See anything defining?"

"No," she said with a sigh. "There was no skin showing. They even had gloves on. And everything was black."

"Right." He capped his pen and looked up at her. "Now want to tell me why in the world you were out here by yourself?"

She saw the concern in his gaze and it snagged at something in her heart. Something untouched in a long time. The feeling that came from someone caring—really caring—about you. It was a good feeling, but also a confusing one coming from Adam.

"I..." She swallowed, knowing that it was best to get it all out in the open. "Today in the shop, one of my fifty-pound bags of flour needed to be hoisted up onto the counter. I came in to find Rosie giving Taylor a hard time about not being able to lift it. I had to help her. It was only fifty pounds, Adam. How in the world would a nineteen year old girl who can't lift a fifty-pound bag of flour get a muscled twenty-something man over that railing?" Margot pointed to the bridge for affect.

Adam's eyebrows rose. "Adrenaline—"

"You're really going to blame this all on adrenaline? And then what about the blood? Where is it? And where are her bloody clothes? It just doesn't add up. Can't you see that?"

Adam took in a sharp breath then placed his hand on her arm, guiding her a few feet away from where techs were going over the area combing for any clues as to who could have pushed Margot.

"Don't you think I've thought of all of these things, Marg?" His expression was so serious, she faltered for a reply. "And don't you think I'm working my hardest to get to the bottom of this to clear your niece?" Even as he said it, he looked around to make sure no one was listening.

"I—"

"No." He placed a finger on her lips to silence her. "I believe she's innocent, but I am searching for justice above all. But you've got to let me do my job and I can't do that if I'm worried that you're out there tracing down leads and placing yourself in danger."

"I'm not in dang—"

"What do you call being shoved into the Potomac?"

She opened her mouth then closed it.

"Please, Margot." Adam's eyes bored into hers. "Be careful."

Part of her snatched at the reality that he wasn't telling her to butt out, only to be careful, but the other part saw the haunted look in his eyes. It was probably the same look she'd given Julian when he left for cases. The one that said *I care too much to have you get hurt.*

"I will," was all she could manage.

He held her gaze longer than necessary then stepped back. "You're free to go, Mrs. Durand."

~

MARGOT GOT home in time to find Taylor raiding the kitchen for a snack. Her eyes grew wide when she took in her disheveled, wet appearance and borrowed muck boots.

"Take a swim, Aunt Margot?"

"Not exactly." She relayed what had happened, again leaving out the reason for her walk, as Taylor's eyes grew to the size of Danishes.

"No way! They went after you? But…but doesn't that like, clear me or something?"

Margot gave her niece a rueful smile. "There's no connection to the case and me being shoved over a wall. What makes you think there is?"

She could tell her question threw her niece for a loop. "I— uh, oh, I don't know. You were…by the bridge, right? The one they found the body below. Made sense that it was about the murder then."

Taylor had recovered, but barely.

"Mind if I watch some TV?"

Margot shook her head. "No. Go ahead. I'm going to work on a new recipe in the kitchen."

"Cool." Taylor grabbed the bowl of popcorn and a diet soda and went to the living room. The sounds of a television sitcom soon floated into the kitchen as Margot leaned up against the counter. After a day in jail and being out on bail, Taylor seemed awfully relaxed about everything. Was her cavalier nature due to the fact that she knew she hadn't done anything wrong, or was it something more…dangerous? A mental disability perhaps?

Margot rubbed her temples. She was jumping to conclusions—ones that involved the thought of her niece being guilty—and that wasn't acceptable. She *knew* the girl. Not well, but she did know her enough to be assured of the fact that she wasn't a psychopathic killer.

She turned her attention to the stack of papers on the counter that contained her notes for a few new recipes she wanted to introduce into the bakery. She moved some aside and noticed that Taylor had left her phone on the counter. She went to pick it up but hesitated. This wasn't the same phone she'd been using before she was arrested…or was it?

Margot turned it over in her hands and frowned. Taylor's other phone had been black but this one was dark blue. With a glance to the entrance of the kitchen, she pressed the home button and the phone flashed to light. One swipe opened the phone and she could see that it looked like any young person's phone. Full of apps and a background photo of the beach.

Another glance to make sure she was alone and Margot pressed the application button for the text messages. She remembered Adam's conversation about not having a connection between Taylor and Marco. Margot had believed it was because there wasn't one, but what if they just couldn't find a trail due to not having all the right information—or the right phone.

Margot was sure they had traced this phone number and all of Taylor's contacts, but she needed to see for herself.

She typed in *Marco* into the messages search bar. Nothing came up.

Then she typed in Lorenzo.

Holding her breath, she pressed enter and waited.

Nothing.

Releasing her breath, she closed the app and put the phone back on the counter. Then, thinking better of it, she walked toward the living room only to stop in the doorway. Taylor was asleep, bowl of popcorn forgotten by her side and the TV blaring.

Margot knew the instant the idea came into her mind that she was going to regret this one way or the other. Either it would work to help prove Taylor's innocence or it could bring up evidence of a connection between Taylor and the crime. Either way, when she slipped noiselessly down the hall to Taylor's room, her motive was justice, not snooping. At least that was what she told herself.

She placed the blue phone on the small bookshelf and turned toward the bed. First she checked under the pillows, then in the drawer, then under the mattress until her hand slid onto something cold, solid, and the shape of a phone.

Heart pounding, Margot looked at the door then pulled the phone out. It slid easily into the palm of her hand and looked identical to the blue phone, differing only in color. No wonder she'd thought it was the same phone.

But why did Taylor have two phones?

Stepping to the door, Margot stuck her head outside and then rushed across the hall to her room. She'd rather be caught in there than in Taylor's room, as long as she had time enough to replace the phone under the mattress.

Then, sitting in her bathroom with the door locked, she pressed the power button. The phone came on. The lock screen picture was of Dillon and Renee. Margot's smile was immediate at seeing the happy, in-love look on her sister's face. How sweet of Taylor to have that on her phone. Scratch that—her second phone.

She swiped right to unlock it, breathing out a sigh of relief when it didn't require a password. This phone was much different than Taylor's other one. It had almost no apps except for one about the stock exchange, a news outlet app, and then a twitter account. The thing that threw Margot off was the lock screen picture. It was of an oilrig in the middle of the ocean. Was this for Taylor to remember her father?

She found the messages icon and tapped it. Many came up, but the names drew Margo's suspicion. Especially the one named, *Honey Bear*.

Tapping on it, she could tell right away that Taylor hadn't written these messages. There was no abbreviated text like Taylor used, and...something caught her attention. The phrase "like a kite caught in a rainstorm" made her catch her breath. That was something Margot had only heard Renee say.

Then the pieces began to slip into place. This was Dillon's phone. She remembered Renee explaining that, when he was on the oilrig, phone service was non-existent most of the time so he often relied on his computer and Wi-Fi to communicate with her. The only explanation was that he'd left his phone at home and Taylor had been using it to text... Who? Who would she text?

Margot scrolled through the contacts but nothing stood out. Then, as she was about to go back to the messages to see what she could find, a text popped up. It only registered a phone number with a local area code for North Bank. Interesting. She memorized the number then pulled down the notifications tab at the top, reading the short message:

MEET ME TONIGHT? <3

MARGOT'S PULSE RACED. She wouldn't risk tipping Taylor off to the fact she'd found the phone by opening—or deleting—the message. As badly as she wanted to, she knew what she had to do.

CHAPTER 12

*T*he night was quiet though windy as Margot pulled on a black sweatshirt while keeping an ear out for any sound that Taylor was still awake. Or worse yet...sneaking out. Margot hated the thought that she'd have to sneak out to follow her niece, but she'd thought of all of the alternatives and this was the best option.

Adam would have a fit if he knew her plans, but in all reality, a teen—even one over the legal age—entrusted to her care was *her* responsibility. If there had been any indication it had something to do with the case, she would have told him, but it didn't. The heart at the end of the message ensured that.

Just then the faint squeak of a window hinge drew her attention to her own open window. They were almost on opposite sides of the house, but she could still hear the window scraping open and the residual crunch of leaves on the trellis that led up to the window.

Pulse racing, Margot slipped from her room, careful to close her door again, and ran to the door. Slipping outside, she hid in the shadows, thankful for her full black wardrobe, and waited to see where Taylor would go once she was clear of the house.

The girl landed with a light thump and paused, taking in the surrounding area. She looked back up at her window then turned toward the steps that led to the street. Margot followed at a careful distance, watching where she stepped and staying in the shadows where possible.

North Bank wasn't a large town, nor had it ever been scary—even at night. It was filled with small town charm and nice people. This close to Washington, D.C., it was a little bit of an anomaly, but she liked that fact. She could get into the city and see the museums when she wanted without the hectic nature of the city *or* the exorbitant price tag that row houses came with. North Bank suited her just fine.

On a night like tonight though, she wasn't so sure it felt as safe as she'd initially thought. Around every corner lurked the possibility of a murderer. Every car driving past could contain a threat. Even a cat running across her path made her cover her mouth so a scream wouldn't escape.

She felt foolish, but her nerves were on edge following

her niece to who knew where to meet some person—presumably a young man—with who knew *what* intent.

Taylor turned up a street Margot recognized. Were they going to the senior center? Frowning, she followed but kept her distance. When her niece got to the center, she checked her phone—presumably the black one that was actually her father's—and slipped around the side of the building. The back side met the sloping hill of a cliff and Margot elected to take the upper ground where bushes would cover her presence. Though that meant she needed to be even more careful to not make noise that would attract Taylor's attention.

Her focus was so intent that, by the time she got close enough to Taylor, another person had arrived.

Lorenzo!

Margot pressed her lips together to keep in her gasp of surprise, but then again, was it really that surprising? She had known Lorenzo was mixed up in this some how, but *how* in the world had he gotten involved with Taylor, let alone gotten her phone number? Margot had been with her ever since she arrived—well, almost.

"What's going on?" Taylor said, stepping closer to the boy than Margot approved of.

"You texted me. Said you wanted to meet." His voice was low, the hint of an accent still lingering there. If Margot remembered correctly, he had come over from Italy with his mother, who was back there now for the summer.

"Um, no," Taylor said, her hands now clasping his, "*You* texted me, you dork." She giggled and went up on tiptoes to give him a quick kiss.

Margot felt her blood boil. This girl was never leaving the house again.

"No," he said, pulling back. In the dim light from the streetlight in the parking lot, Margot could see the frown on his face. "*You* texted me."

"No—" Taylor was frowning now, looking confused.

"Whatever…" He shrugged, wrapping his arms around her and pulling her close. "I guess whoever texted who, this was a good idea."

Margot rolled her eyes. She was about to bust this little meeting up, when something in their conversation drew out her suspicion. Neither one of them admitted to having texted the other. Why would either of them lie? And, from what she'd seen on Taylor's second phone, she *hadn't* texted him. Why would Lorenzo lie about texting her? He obviously was happy to see her. It made no sense.

A chill raced up her spine. Something wasn't right about this meeting.

Her gaze shot back to the couple then to the surrounding area shadowed in darkness. The back wall of the center was blank, no windows or doors, then she looked the way they'd come in. Nothing but the faint light filtering in from the parking lot's street light. Then, with a shallow breath, she looked to the other side of the building. It was much darker there, covered by a tall oak tree and mostly hidden from light by the bulk of the building.

Movement caught her eye. There was definitely something—or someone—there. Heart hammering in her chest, Margot sneaked around the bush, closer to the couple but also to get a better view. It was so dark she couldn't be certain, but it looked like an arm holding a gun had snaked around the corner.

Now her palms were sweating and she was positive she was hyperventilating. The couple was too distracted to notice, but Margot was positive they were the killer's targets.

Margot felt the press of an invisible hand on her back pushing her forward to do something. She had to time it just right, but she would have no indication when the killer would strike. Then again, if she didn't act soon, it could be too late.

In a rush of adrenaline, Margot jumped forward, off the higher ground and toward the couple, yelling, "Get down!"

The minute she connected with both Lorenzo and Taylor, sending them toppling down, a gunshot rang out through the night.

"What—" Lorenzo cried out.

"Ahhh," Taylor screamed.

Shaking, Margot grabbed Taylor. "It's me, Tay. It's Margot."

Her niece stopped fighting but Lorenzo jumped up, looking down at Taylor and then, before any of them could say anything, he ran off and disappeared into the night.

~

MARGOT PLACED a hot cup of tea on the coffee table in front of her niece and then handed the other to Adam.

"Thanks." He looked between the women, his frustration evident. "My officers didn't find the shooter—only one bullet casing and an unfortunate tree that seemed to be the recipient of the kill shot."

Taylor flinched at the word kill.

"Adam—"

"I should have taken you both back to the station for questioning," he cut in, the tension in his shoulders easing only slightly, "but the chief said you'd been through enough for one night."

Margot turned her gaze to her niece. Tears streaked her face and a light bruise marred her pretty features, but thankfully, that was the worst of it.

"It could have been much worse," Margot said.

Adam nodded and turned to look at the girl as well.

"I'm sorry," Taylor whispered, staring down into the cup.

"Taylor," Margot cut in, cradling her own cup of tea to eat away the coldness that seemed to sink to her core. "You've got to tell us what's going on. No more of this bottling things up and keeping secrets. You were almost killed tonight." The words sent more icy shivers down her spine.

Another tear streaked down Taylor's cheek and she sniffed, wiping it away with the back of her hand.

"I care about you. I just... I guess I don't know what to do. Maybe I should just have your mom come out and—"

"No." Taylor looked up, first at Margot then to Adam. "I'll tell you everything."

Margot met her gaze.

"Please—just don't call Renee. Not yet."

Margot felt somehow dishonest for threatening to call Taylor's mother, but the suggestion had gotten her the results she'd hoped for.

"Level with me, Taylor." Adam's tone left no room for argument and she saw the girl deflate a little. "How do you know Lorenzo?"

"Okay." She wiped her eyes again, then steeled herself with a deep breath, "When Dad told me that I was coming out to North Bank for the summer, I wasn't happy. I mean, you can guess why, right?"

"Yes," Margot agreed.

"Getting up at three in the morning every day is such a bummer. Anyway, I wasn't really into it all, but I thought, you know, that I could make the best of it. So...I kind of borrowed my dad's phone and got on a dating app. I put in the North Bank area and ended up meeting someone on the app."

"Lorenzo," Margot guessed, feeling Adam's gaze on her.

"Yeah. And, Aunt Margot, no matter what you think, you're wrong. He's a nice guy. We hit it off and started chatting via text. It actually made me excited to come out here, you know?"

Margot bit her cheek to keep from saying anything. They needed to hear the whole truth before she gave her two cents.

"Go on," Margot said.

"I honestly don't know what happened, though. When we went to that Italian restaurant that first night, the waiter —Marco—slipped me a note. He said he knew Lorenzo and wanted to meet with me about him. I thought... I don't know, I thought he knew where I could meet up with Lorenzo because I hadn't heard back from him since I'd landed. So I went to talk with him..."

Margot leaned forward, her stomach clenching. "Why did he attack you?"

"That's just it. When I went back there, he was all flirty. I mean, yeah, he's handsome and I flirted a little too, but I didn't get why he'd do that if he was friends with Lorenzo and knew we were texting. But then he asked me where 'it' was. I had *no* idea what he was talking about. I told him that, but he didn't believe me. He said Lorenzo said I would give it to him."

"He didn't say what it was he was looking for?" Adam interjected.

"No!" Taylor blew out a stream of air and shook her head. "Sorry, he just made me really mad. I told him I had no idea what he was talking about and that's when he grabbed me and shook me as if I'd drop it loose or something." She rolled her eyes. "That's when you came in Aunt Margot—thankfully."

"Then he came back outside to what? Convince you again?" Adam's hazel eyes focused intently on the girl.

"I guess." Taylor took a sip of her tea.

Margot considered the facts. Replaying the scene in her mind, she tried to remember the exact situation when she burst into the janitor's closet. She had assumed they were locked in an amorous embrace, but it could have been like Taylor explained.

But that didn't explain how Taylor's prints had gotten on the knife.

"Did you use a knife at the restaurant?" Even as she asked the question, she met Adam's gaze.

"Margot..." he cautioned.

126

"A knife? No, I don't think—" Taylor frowned, her eyes searching the ceiling to remember. "Wait. I didn't use one, but I did unroll the silverware from the napkin and I'm sure I touched it—" She stopped, her eyes widening. "I *did* touch it. Oh my goodness, do you think…" She looked at Adam and Margot felt her gaze trail to him as well.

He let out a sigh and nodded. "It was confirmed that the knife was from Antonio's."

Taylor's eyes grew large, but Margot cut her off before she could say anything. "Tay, honey, I know that you didn't kill that man, but you kept so much from me—from the police. A whole different phone and a connection to North Bank. Why didn't you say something?"

Taylor cringed, cupping her tea between both hands. "I was just afraid I'd get Lorenzo in trouble. He's working so hard to get his accounting degree and…" She shrugged. "I like him."

"So that was him you were meeting with at the senior center?"

Taylor nodded and Margot let out a breath. Adam nodded in her peripheral vision.

"All right," he said, running his hand along his pants. "That's enough for tonight. Why don't you two ladies get some rest?" He met Margot's gaze. "I've stationed an officer outside the house for tonight, just in case."

Taylor put her tea down and rubbed her arms.

"Thank you," Margot said, standing. "Why don't you go on to bed, honey?"

Taylor nodded and left for her room as Adam stood as well.

"What did I tell you about being careful?" His gaze was hard and unblinking.

"I know," Margot clutched her arms, feeling cold as well. "It was foolish but I didn't think the text had anything to do with the case."

"Right." Adam didn't sound convinced. The silence stretched out until he spoke up again. "Look, I shouldn't do this, but…I'll be going by Antonio's again tomorrow to review his security tapes. Maybe something will jog your memory. Want to join me?"

She'd been prepared for a scolding but instead she'd been invited to join him on case business?

She smiled up at him, feeling hopeful. She would find something on those tapes—she had to.

"Well, Detective Eastwood, it looks like the bakery is going to be closed tomorrow."

CHAPTER 13

*E*ven though she had the luxury of sleeping in, Margot's body didn't think too highly of that. She hadn't woken up at three, but five o'clock rolled around and, despite her exhaustion, she couldn't convince herself to go back to sleep.

Rising, she dressed and did her morning exercises, riding her stationary bike and going through the motions for her next Krav Maga class. Then she showered and decided it was a good morning to make crêpes.

Soon, the smells of Nutella, strawberries and cream, and apple cinnamon-filled crêpes scented the air.

"It smells so good in here," Taylor said, coming into the kitchen with her hair in a messy ponytail and still in her PJs.

"Thought you might enjoy some crêpes."

"You're seriously the best, Aunt Marg!"

Margot handed her niece a cup of coffee and a plate, and soon they were both enjoying the sweet crêpes.

"What's going on today?" Taylor asked, looking a little wary. Was she wondering if she had to go back to the police station?

During her early morning, Margot had thought long and hard about what she would do with Taylor while she and Adam were at Antonio's. It felt foolish thinking of her niece like she was a child needing babysitting, but it was more than that. So far, despite her honesty the night before, she still had kept things from them. In order to keep her safe, and above suspicion, Margot had decided something.

"I'm taking you to hang out with Bentley today."

"Bentley—wait, that old guy who always orders the caramel pecan cinnamon roll and a cup of coffee?"

Margot frowned at her use of 'old guy,' but nodded. "Yes. He's a very nice *elderly* gentleman and I'm sure he can put you to good use at the senior center."

The young girl frowned. Was she thinking about the night before?

"Don't worry," Margot was quick to add. "I talked with Adam and he's going to have an officer accompany you for the day."

"Am I in trouble?"

Margot almost laughed. Did she mean aside from the murder charge? Then again, it was good that she was so confident in her own innocence. Margot was too, increasingly so as more of the facts began to line up.

"Just trust me on this. It'll be good for you to spend some time with Bentley and you'll be protected."

She nodded, taking a bite of a Nutella-filled crêpe. "Hey, Aunt Margot?"

Margot stopped collecting the dirty dishes from the table to look down at her niece. "Yes?"

"Thanks." Her cheeks colored. "For, you know, believing in me. Renee thinks the worst of me all the time. I think she would have freaked out if she were here, but you've been really cool about all of this."

Margot wasn't sure 'cool' was the term to describe how she'd felt, but she nodded and accepted the girl's thanks. "You're welcome. But, Taylor, can I tell you something?" Taylor nodded and Margot sat back down, leaning against the table.

"Despite what you may think, your mom loves you. A lot. And I'm not just saying that because she's my sister. When we have our calls, she always spends at least half of them talking about you and Dillon. She cares so much for you both. And I think you and I both know she would never try to replace your mother."

"Yeah…" Taylor looked down at her plate. "I know she cares. I guess…I don't know. It's easier pushing her away, just in case…"

Margot leaned forward. "In case you lose her too?"

When Taylor looked up, she was shocked to see tears in her niece's eyes. "Yeah. It hurt bad enough losing one mom, I just don't want to lose another."

Margot reached out and placed her hand over the girl's. "I know, sweetie, but don't you think by holding back you're missing out on something? Like a second chance at having a mom again?"

Taylor sniffed and wiped under her eyes. "Maybe you're right."

Words bubbled up to the surface, but Margot held them back. Taylor didn't need someone telling her what to do, she needed to decide it for herself.

"We leave in half an hour. Think you'll be ready?"

As if grateful to have a chance to slip away, Taylor nodded and padded down the hall to her room while Margot cleaned up the dishes.

They left, Margot noting the plainclothes officer who followed them, and arrived at the senior center right on time. As if he'd been waiting for them, Bentley came out side. "Hiya, Taylor," he said, nodding to her niece.

"Hi," she said, looking oddly shy.

"Listen," he said to Taylor as she got out of the car, "we're going to get along just fine. I promise I won't bore you with old stories...that is, unless you'd be interested in hearing about some of the cases I tried."

"Cases?" Taylor's interest was piqued.

"I was a lawyer," Bentley said with a grin.

"That'd be cool."

"Good. Talking with you will get me out of the next fundraiser Kim Penberthy has planned."

Margot leaned forward. "*Another* fundraiser?"

Bentley shook his head. "Yeah. Figures. But this time, I'm keeping track." He patted his pocket where she could see the top of a notebook sticking out. "No one's going to pull the wool over old Bentley's eyes. Come on, kid, let's go."

"I'll be back in an hour, two tops," Margot said, then rolled up the window.

Bentley waved a hand at her in farewell and she pulled out of the parking lot, glad to see the officer's car parked there. She breathed out a sigh and thought of her conversation with Bentley that morning. He'd drilled her on what she'd found out about the missing money, but the pieces still weren't there. She needed to talk to Lorenzo, but after last night, she had a feeling he was laying low if the police hadn't already caught up with him. Then again, what could they hold him on? What was his part in all of this? Aside from his connection to Taylor, of course.

Then again... Her eyes narrowed as she pulled up in front of the police station. Neither Taylor or Lorenzo had admitted to texting one another. Was it possible the texts were fake? But who were they from?

A tap on her window nearly made her scream until she saw Adam's smiling face.

"A bit jumpy this morning, huh?" he said when she rolled down the window.

"If your niece had been the one shot at last night, you'd be jumpy too."

His expression sobered and he circled around to get in the passenger seat.

"What are you doing?"

"Mind if we take your car?" His grin returned and he held up the two coffees. "Had a feeling you'd need another one of these."

She let his easygoing demeanor sooth her and she accepted the coffee from him.

"To Antonio's," Adam said, holding up his coffee as if pointing the way. She rolled her eyes at his obvious good mood.

"How are you so awake?"

"It's all an illusion," he said, a smile in his voice. "That and caffeine. Does wonders on the mood."

As if to prove his theory she took a long sip of her coffee. "Black. Just the way I like it."

"I know."

The familiar statement caused something to stir in her, but she pushed it aside. They were hopefully going to get some answers today while at Antonio's. They had to, because the case against Taylor, while not error-proof, didn't offer many alternatives.

"Answer me this," she said, hoping he would be able to. "Have you talked to Lorenzo?"

"Business as usual, huh, Marge?" She smiled at the nickname only Adam used for her. It had annoyed her to no end at first, but now—though she'd never admit it to him—it had grown on her. "Can't a man have a moment's peace in a car ride?"

"No. Now spill it."

Sighing as if giving up, Adam straightened in his seat. "We can't find him. We've checked the apartment rented out in his name, I talked with Antonio on the phone last night—poor guy, definitely woke him up—and canvassed his neighborhood. No one knows where he is."

"Do you suspect him?"

"I'm requisitioning his phone records, should have something this morning. I also put in an order for your niece's *other* phone. I'm not sure what to think of our boy

Lorenzo. He's involved—if only by association with Taylor—but beyond that I don't know."

"He was doing accounting for the senior center."

"What?"

She filled Adam in on her conversation with Bentley and then Eve, explaining the phone call she'd made to the professor.

"So, not the brightest candle in the class but is he smart enough to 'cook the books,' if I can use that term?"

"It doesn't feel right," Margot said, drumming her fingers on the steering wheel as they pulled into Antonio's nearly empty parking lot. She turned to look at Adam when they'd come to a stop. "I don't know him, so I could be wrong, but from what I've heard people say about him, he's a good kid, going to night school to become an accountant and working part time for his uncle. Aside from being friends with the murder victim and dating the suspected murderer, I'm not sure how he fits into all of this."

Adam nodded slowly then put his hand on the door handle. "Let me think about it."

She climbed out and followed him into the empty restaurant. The only person she saw was Antonio sitting in one of the booths with sun streaming in through the window. He rose when they entered and came toward them, his smile lacking the brightness it usually did.

"Hello, *mia bella.*" He kissed her on the cheek. "Detective."

"We'd like to take another look at those security tapes."

"*Si.* Right. Of course. This way."

Margot sent Adam a worried look, but he didn't seem to notice, or he ignored her. Poor Antonio.

"I am saddened by the absence of my nephew. It is not like him. He is a good boy," Antonio said as they walked down the hall to his office. He was a man who wore his heart on his sleeve, but still, it hurt to see him so upset.

"I'm so sorry, Antonio."

He waved a hand and ushered them into the room. "Here are the cameras. They face the parking lot, the door, and one view of the cash register. I had them installed after a robbery several years ago."

"Thanks, Antonio. I can run this if you have things to do."

The man nodded and shuffled out of the office, shoulders drooping.

"Poor man," Margot said.

"Yes, but I'm not so sure *he* isn't involved."

"What?" Margot was shocked Adam could even think Antonio was somehow involved in all of this.

"Margot..." Adam's tone held a warning. "You can't look at anyone in a case as a friend. They're all suspects."

"Am I a suspect?" she challenged, meeting his gaze and sure her cheeks were flushed at the heat of passion she felt for the fact that Antonio was innocent.

"No." He held her gaze for a long time and looked like he wanted to say more, but the screen flickered and drew their attention back to the monitor.

"That's the table we sat at that night," Margot observed. "The one Antonio's in now."

Adam sat down and began pressing buttons and turning dials. "Interesting," he said to himself.

"What?"

"When we were here last, we focused on the parking lot. We saw Marco come toward Taylor, saw her push him away, and that was that. I didn't even *think* to watch you *in* the restaurant. I'm sure a tech did, but do you mind watching through it?"

Her confidence boosted at his belief she might see something they missed, she nodded and leaned over to watch. He slowed the tape down when one camera picked up her car pulling in. They ran through them being seated at their table and then he let it play through.

Margot watched intently, seeing Marco come up to the table several times, even catching when he slipped the note to Taylor, and then she saw Taylor bolt from the table after slipping a note into her pocket. Next, she walked past two tables and—

"Wait," she said, peering closer at the screen.

"What? What do you see?"

Realization washed through Margot as the pieces began to fit together like a perfect puzzle. She knew who had murdered Marco—but could she prove it?

CHAPTER 14

*M*argot's heart raced as Adam, driving her car, sped from Antonio's restaurant toward the senior center. She couldn't exactly explain the feeling of needing to rush to Taylor, but something told her that the killer wasn't about to sit by and wait for them to discover their identity.

"Are you sure about this, Marge?" Adam said, his hands clutching the steering wheel as if his racing through the streets was the most natural thing in the world.

"I'm positive."

They careened around a corner. They were almost to the center now.

"We don't exactly have proof."

She tapped her foot on the carpeted floor. It was true. Though the surveillance tape didn't show the killer's face, it had shown enough for Margot to recognize who had taken the knife from their table and then slipped out the front door.

Adam shot into the parking lot and skidded to a stop out front. This was it. The moment of truth.

"I want you to wait in the car while I—"

"Absolutely not."

He looked at her as if she'd lost her mind. "You're not going in there, Margot."

"Yes. I am." Her gaze left no room for argument. "I've got to get to my niece. I'll be fine."

His shoulders slumped. "Let me radio my officer first."

Hand on the door, she waited.

"Yes, sir?" came a crackly reply.

Adam nodded toward her and she slipped from the car. She knew Adam wouldn't be far behind, but she was more concerned with finding Taylor. They needed to get her to safety before the killer made her their next target.

The recreational space at the front was almost empty, only a few seniors occupying the chairs around the perimeter, and she raced toward Bentley's favorite spot. Sliding on the slick floor, she rushed around the corner and came to a halt. It was empty.

Where were they?

She ran through the logical areas they could be. They weren't in the rec space, and they weren't in the reading room she'd passed on the way to this spot...then she heard voices at the end of the hallway where the office was. She couldn't make out the words, but the tone was harsh. It sent a thrill of fear through Margot.

Sliding out her phone, she shot a text to Adam and then followed the sound.

"I—I don't get it. What's going on?"

Margot's heart shot to her throat. It was Taylor's voice, thin and high.

"Come on, Taylor," Bentley said. "Just stand next to me."

"That's right," a woman's voice said. "Stand right there."

Margot's stomach clenched. Just as she'd expected. It was Kim Penberthy.

"Now if you'll just—"

"I don't think so, Kim," Margot said, coming around the corner into a possibly hostile scene.

Kim stood next to a desk, a silver revolver in her hand aimed at Bentley and Taylor.

Oh, God! Keep them safe!

"Isn't that just like you, Margot. Sticking your nose into everyone's business."

Margot fought the urge to lunge to get the gun away from

the crazy woman. It would do no good to startle her, since her finger rested lightly on the trigger.

"Just hold on there, Kim," she said, raising her hands in a defensive position. "No one's going to stop you. Just do what you need to do."

"What I *need* to do? I *need* for this to all be over." She blew out a frustrated breath. "I needed it to be over with Marco's death. That was the plan—and the plan is *always right.*"

Margot started to feel sick. Kim was obviously at a tipping point; if she wasn't already over the edge, she'd be there soon. It wasn't good that she was talking so openly about the situation. Then again, if she could get her to confess… But that would only work if they weren't killed. Where was Adam?

"*You* killed that guy?" Taylor said. Margot shot her a look, but she ignored it. "Why did you blame me?"

Kim shook her head and looked down at the papers spread out before her. In the shuffling, Margot picked up a noise behind her in the hall. Her heart hammered in her chest as she caught a glimpse of something—more like someone—in the reflection of the picture hanging up behind Kim.

It had to be Adam. That or her eyes were playing tricks on her. This was it—her chance.

"She did kill that poor young man," Margot said with

more boldness than she felt. "Because she was being blackmailed."

Kim's head snapped up. The gun lowered and Kim turned it toward Margot. The feeling of its deadly weight pressed against Margot's chest, but she pushed her fear down. She had to focus.

"What do you know about it?"

"I didn't, until I saw the tapes at Antonio's—the ones that show you stealing the knife from Taylor's place setting. Then it all just fell together."

"Oh? Why don't you enlighten me, if you're so smart, Margot Durand."

Hoping it would buy them some time, she pressed forward with what she'd put together. "It started when Eve suggested Lorenzo to you as an accountant for the senior center fundraisers. You're too smart of a woman to just take someone's suggestion, so I have a feeling you followed up on Lorenzo and found out what I did—he wasn't the best in the class by a long shot. I don't know exactly, but I have a feeling you convinced him to let you help him. He probably needed the money and you were all too eager to get your hands on the accounting sheets."

Kim's expression hardened. "Go on, if you're so smart to think you know it all."

"It gets a little murky for me here, but I have a feeling Marco—being the helpful friend that he was—started looking into the discrepancies Lorenzo thought he was seeing. Marco saw an opportunity to blackmail you. I think he wanted to talk to Taylor that night at Antonio's because he was convinced Lorenzo had given her proof of the embezzling. If he got it from Taylor, then he could use it against you." Margot shifted, sneaking a glance at Taylor to see that she was as baffled by all of this as Bentley was. "I'm sure the phone records—and someone tech savvy— will find that the texts Marco got weren't from Lorenzo at all, but from you."

Kim leveled her gaze at Margot, but didn't interrupt. But Margot needed Kim to admit to it or else it was all just conjecture.

"If I remember correctly, you used to work at a phone tech company before you married our illustrious mayor. Maybe you learned a few tricks there. Anyway, I think after that, it's pretty clear. You lured Marco to the bridge —probably with another false text—and used the knife you'd stolen from Taylor's place setting to kill him."

Kim laughed derisively. "Sounds a little too perfect, doesn't it, Marg? Besides, you can't prove I was at Antonio's."

The hard look in the woman's eyes told Margot she somehow knew they couldn't identify her. "But you made a mistake, Kim." The woman shifted, her eyes narrowing. "When you saw me at the senior center the other day, you said you'd seen me *three* times in a week. I didn't think anything of it, but then I realized you had seen me at Antonio's restaurant—that was the third time."

"You're too smart for your own good."

"I'm right, aren't I?" Margot pressed.

"You're right," Kim said, nodding. "But no one will ever hear the truth—from any of you."

Suddenly, Kim shifted, taking a step around the desk and coming toward Margot. "We're going to take a little walk—"

"Stop right there, Kim Penberthy."

Margot gasped as Adam came into the room, his gun trained on the woman. Noise outside the window drew a quick glance and she saw more officers, guns out and trained on Kim.

"You," she said to Margot through clenched teeth. "It would have worked except you couldn't keep your nose out of it." With a huff, she dropped her hand. Adam moved forward in an instant, taking the gun from her and calling in another officer to cuff Kim and read the rights.

Margot turned toward Taylor and Bentley, grasping her niece in a tight hug. "I'm so glad you guys are all right."

"Dang, Aunt Marg, you just faced down a killer."

Despite the scare, Bentley had a small smile on his face. "I knew you'd solve all of this. I just knew it."

CHAPTER 15

Brilliant sunlight shone on the small round tables Margot had forced Adam to drag out from her storage shed. They now sat behind the shop, waiting to invite patrons brave enough to tackle the brisk wind.

Bentley, Taylor, Lorenzo, Adam, and Margot all sat around one such table, sipping coffee, eating pastries, and tugging their coats a little closer.

"You said summer was coming, didn't you, Aunt Marg?"

Margot shook her head, smiling at her niece with her hand wrapped around Lorenzo's. "Eventually."

"She's right, you know," Bentley said. "The sun always comes out. Just takes a little time."

They sat in amiable silence for a few minutes before

Taylor stood, Lorenzo following her lead. "We're going for a walk along the byway. That okay?"

Margot looked between the two. So much had transpired in the last few days, but she knew she couldn't keep Taylor under lock and key every hour of every day.

"Sure, just be back by three. We're leaving then to pick Renee up from the airport."

"I remember," Taylor said. "It'll be nice to see Mom."

At the word 'mom,' Margot felt tears in her eyes but she held them back, pressing her lips closed.

"Thank you, Mrs. Durand," Lorenzo said. "I'll watch out for her."

"And you'll be on your best behavior," Adam added with a stern look. The young man paled and nodded. Margot watched as they took off down the walkway toward Miller's Bridge hand in hand, a smile on her lips.

"Can you believe it?" Bentley said.

Margot laughed and looked at him. "What?"

"Just…all of this. And there they go, happy as two lovers can be."

"It was a bit of a whirlwind, but I'm glad it's over now," Margot agreed.

"Speaking of over," Bentley stood, taking his coffee cup

with him. "I'm going to go harass Rosie for some more coffee."

He shuffled inside and Margot turned to look at Adam. "You're quiet."

His hand rested around his nearly empty cup, but he didn't meet her gaze for a long time. When he did, there was an unreadable expression in his eyes.

"Margot, you gave me the scare of a lifetime."

She swallowed, remembering the face-off with Kim only a few days previous.

"She's behind bars now. I'm safe."

He shrugged. "True. Once we found the text messages she'd sent to Marco, Lorenzo, and Taylor, her case fell into place. We've got several witnesses placing her at Antonio's as well. I still can't believe she was funneling money from the senior center fundraisers into her husband's campaign. But she could have killed you."

Margot felt ice flood her veins. "But she didn't."

"True, but still…"

"She had many chances to do that—like when she was going to murder Lorenzo and blame Taylor that night behind the senior center, but God didn't allow it."

"I know," he said, leaning forward and dropping his hand on top of hers on the metal table. "I just worry about you.

Julian would come back and haunt me if I let anything happen to you."

She smiled, shaking her head. "He would be thankful that I have a good friend like you to solve mysteries with."

Adam grinned, leaning back in his chair. "Speaking of mysteries—how did you know about the connection between Kim and Lorenzo? That the boy wasn't involved."

Margot swallowed and looked away.

"You totally guessed," Adam said, incredulous.

"Can I blame my gut?" She laughed. "When I realized it was Kim in that tape from Antonio's, I started to work back in my mind. She fit into every scenario. She works out a lot so she's strong—strong enough to haul a dead body over Miller's Bridge and strong enough to barrel into me and push me over into the river. Plus, she's always had her hand in the mayor's campaigns and when I saw her at Antonio's asking him to cater a big party, like one for a mayoral election win, I got suspicious."

"But still...that was a leap."

She shrugged. "I knew Taylor was innocent. So once I heard Bentley talking about how Kim was part of the fundraising committee—and her mess-up about how many times she'd seen me that week—I knew that she was the one behind it all. Her husband stood to gain a lot, but she stood to gain more as his wife. Besides, with Marco running "all those errands" and obviously having money like Antonio had said, it made me think he had more going on the side than just a busboy job."

"Still, you took a risk."

"I did." She nodded in agreement. "But, Adam, just like you won't sit on the sidelines when you know that there's a bad guy out there, I couldn't sit by and do nothing when I knew Taylor was innocent."

He opened his mouth to speak but then closed it, his frown deepening.

"What, Detective Eastwood?"

The corner of his mouth quirked. "I just don't like the thought of you being in danger."

His words reminded her of Julian. He'd always been so protective. But there was a truth that she'd always held on to when she thought about her husband being in harm's way and she felt the urge to share that with Adam now.

"Adam, we can't live our lives afraid. You don't do that when you charge into a heated situation and I couldn't let fear rule me from stepping in to help my niece and Bentley. I have to trust that God will protect me and give me the strength to stand up and speak when the time is right."

"I just wish that guns weren't involved when the time was right."

She couldn't help her smile. "I'd prefer they be left out of the situation as well."

He held her gaze for a moment longer, then nodded once. "I understand. Just promise me you'll always be careful."

"I wouldn't be anything else."

"Who want's more coffee?" Bentley said, coming back out to the patio with a carafe in one hand and an éclair in the other.

"You're going to eat me out of house and bakery," Margot said, holding up her cup.

The older man smiled and wagged his eyebrows. "Probably, but what a way to go."

They all shared in a laugh and Margot sat back, enjoying the warmth of the sun on her back and the warmth of the company that surrounded her. Just like Bentley had said, the sun always did come out—just like the truth. Sometimes it just took a little time and a little investigating.

~

Thanks for reading *Croissants and Corruption*. I hope you enjoyed reading the story as much as I enjoyed writing it. If you did, it would be awesome if you left a review for me on Amazon and/or Goodreads.

If you would like to know about future cozy mysteries by me and the other authors at Fairfield Publishing, make sure to sign up for our Cozy Mystery Newsletter. We will send you our FREE Cozy Mystery Starter Library just for signing up. All the details are on the next page.

As a special surprise, I have included recipes for some of the treats that were featured in the book. You will find those recipes right after the newsletter information.

Lastly, at the very end of the book, I have included a couple previews of books by friends and fellow authors at Fairfield Publishing. First is a preview of *Up in Smoke* by Shannon VanBergen - it's the first book in the Glock Grannies Cozy Mystery series. Second is a preview of *A Pie to Die For* by Stacey Alabaster - it's part of the popular Bakery Detectives Cozy Mystery series. I really hope you like the samples. If you do, both books are available on Amazon.

- Get Up in Smoke here:
  amazon.com/dp/B06XHKYRRX

- Get A Pie to Die For here:
  amazon.com/dp/B01D6ZVT78

FAIRFIELD COZY MYSTERY NEWSLETTER

Make sure you sign up for the Fairfield Cozy Mystery Newsletter so you can keep up with our latest releases. When you sign up, **we will send you our FREE Cozy Mystery Starter Library!**

FairfieldPublishing.com/cozy-newsletter/

After you sign up to get your Free Starter Library, turn the page and check out the free previews :)

RECIPES

PERFECT COCONUT MACAROONS

*S*ervings: 26 macaroons

PREP TIME: 20 Minutes

Cook Time: 25 Minutes

Total Time: 45 Minutes

INGREDIENTS

- 5-1/3 cups (one 14-ounce bag) sweetened shredded coconut
- ¾ cup plus 2 tablespoons sweetened condensed milk (not evaporated milk; also don't be tempted to use the whole can. Trust me!)
- 1 teaspoon vanilla extract

- 2 large eggs whites
- 1/4 teaspoon salt
- 4 ounces semi-sweet chocolate, best quality such as Ghirardelli, chopped (optional)

Instructions

- Preheat the oven to 325°F. Put two oven racks near the center of the oven. Line two baking sheets with parchment paper.
- In a medium bowl, mix together the shredded coconut, sweetened condensed milk and vanilla extract. Set aside.
- In the bowl of an electric mixer, beat the egg whites and salt until stiff peaks form. Use a large rubber spatula to fold the egg whites into the coconut mixture.
- Using two spoons, form heaping tablespoons of the mixture into mounds on the prepared baking sheets, spacing about 1 inch apart. Bake for 23 to 25 minutes, rotating the pans from top to bottom and front to back, until the tops and edges are golden. Let cool on the pans for a few minutes, then transfer to a wire rack to cook completely.
- If dipping the macaroons in chocolate, melt the chocolate in a microwave-safe bowl at medium power, stopping and stirring at 30 second intervals, until just smooth and creamy. (Alternatively, melt the chocolate in a double boiler over simmering water.) Dip the bottoms of

the macaroons in the chocolate, letting any excess drip back into the bowl, and return to the lined baking sheets. Place the macaroons in the refrigerator for about 10 minutes to allow the chocolate to set. The cookies keep well in an airtight container at room temperature for about a week.

EASY CHOCOLATE HAZELNUT CRESCENT ROLLS

Servings: varies by package

INGREDIENTS

1 can Pillsbury Crescent rolls (in the tube from the refrigerator section of your grocery store – not the frozen kind)

Nutella

Chocolate Chips

Preheat oven to 375. Cover cookie sheet with parchment paper.

ROLL out each crescent roll and smooth on a layer of Nutella. Don't get it too close to the edges – also don't be stingy here, put on a nice layer of that hazelnut chocolatey goodness.

Sprinkle on chocolate chips (Use as many as you like. I usually sprinkle 12- 15 on each roll)

Roll loosely (look at picture on back of tube to see how to roll properly)

Bake according to the directions on the back of the crescent roll packing.

These are great for breakfast or dessert!

BOOK PREVIEWS

I could feel my hair puffing up like cotton candy in the humidity as I stepped outside the Miami airport. I pushed a sticky strand from my face, and I wished for a minute that it were a cheerful pink instead of dirty blond, just to complete the illusion.

"Thank you so much for picking me up from the airport." I smiled at the sprightly old lady I was struggling to keep up with. "But why did you say my grandmother couldn't pick me up?"

"I didn't say." She turned and gave me a toothy grin— clearly none of them original—and winked. "I parked over here."

When we got to her car, she opened the trunk and threw in the sign she had been holding when she met me in baggage claim. The letters were done in gold glitter glue and she had drawn flowers with markers all around the edges. My name "Nikki Rae Parker" flashed when the sun reflected off of them, temporarily blinding me.

"I can tell you put a lot of work into that sign." I carefully put my luggage to the side of it, making sure not to touch her sign—partially because I didn't want to crush it and partially because it didn't look like the glue had dried yet.

"Well, your grandmother didn't give me much time to make it. I only had about ten minutes." She glanced at the sign proudly before closing the trunk. She looked me in the eyes. "Let's get on the road. We can chit chat in the car."

With that, she climbed in and clicked on her seat belt. As I got in, she was applying a thick coat of bright red lipstick while looking in the rearview mirror. "Gotta look sharp in case we get pulled over." She winked again, her heavily wrinkled eyelid looking like it thought about staying closed before it sprung back up again.

I thought about her words for a moment. She must get

pulled over a lot, I thought. Poor old lady. I could picture her going ten miles an hour while the rest of Miami flew by her.

"Better buckle up." She pinched her lips together before blotting them slightly on a tissue. She smiled at me and for a moment, I was jealous of her pouty lips, every line filled in by layers and layers of red.

I did as I was told and buckled my seat belt before I sunk down into her caramel leather seats. I was exhausted, both physically and mentally, from the trip. I closed my eyes and tried to forget my troubles, taking in a deep breath and letting it out slowly to give all my worry and fear ample time to escape my body. For the first time since I had made the decision to come here, I felt at peace. Unfortunately, it was short-lived.

The sound of squealing tires filled the air and my eyes flung open to see this old lady zigzagging through the parking garage. She took the turns without hitting the brakes, hugging each curve like a racecar driver. When we exited the garage and turned onto the street, she broke out in laughter. "That's my favorite part!"

I tugged my seat belt to make sure it was on tight. This was not going to be the relaxing drive I had thought it would be.

We hit the highway and I felt like I was in an arcade game. She wove in and out of traffic at a speed I was sure matched her old age.

"Ya know, the older I get the worse other people drive." She took one hand off the wheel and started to rummage through her purse, which sat between us.

"Um, can I help you with something?" My nerves were starting to get the best of me as her eyes were focused more on her purse than the road.

"Oh no, I've got it. I'm sure it's in here somewhere." She dug a little more, pulling out a package of AA batteries and then a ham sandwich.

Brake lights lit up in front of us and I screamed, bracing myself for impact. The old woman glanced up and pulled the car to the left in a quick jerk before returning to her purse. Horns blared from behind us.

"There it is!" She pulled out a package of wintergreen Life Savers. "Do you want one?"

"No, thank you." I could barely get the words out.

"I learned a long time ago that it was easier if I just drove and did my thing instead of worrying about what all the other drivers were doing. It's easier for them to get out of my way instead of me getting out of theirs. My reflexes aren't what they used to be." She popped a mint in her mouth and smiled. "I love wintergreen. I don't know why peppermint is more popular. Peppermint is so stuffy; wintergreen is fun."

She seemed to get in a groove with her driving and soon my grip was loosening on the sides of the seat, the blood slowly returning to my knuckles. Suddenly I realized I hadn't asked her name.

"I was so confused when you picked me up from the airport instead of my Grandma Dean that I never asked your name."

She didn't respond, just kept her eyes on the road with a steely look on her face. I was happy to see her finally being serious about driving, so I turned to look out the window. "It's beautiful here," I said after a few minutes of silence. I turned to look at her again and noticed that she was still focused straight ahead. I stared at her for a moment and realized she never blinked. Panic rose through my chest.

"Ma'am!" I shouted as I leaned forward to take the wheel. "Are you okay?"

She suddenly sprung to action, screaming and jerking the wheel to the left. Her screaming caused me to scream and I grabbed the wheel and pulled it to the right, trying to get us back in our lane. We continued to scream until the car stopped teetering and settled down to a nice hum on the road.

"Are you trying to kill us?" The woman's voice was hoarse and she seemed out of breath.

"I tried to talk to you and you didn't answer!" I practically shouted. "I thought you had a heart attack or something!"

"You almost gave me one!" She flashed me a dirty look.

"And you made me swallow my mint. You're lucky I didn't choke to death!"

"I'm sorry." As I said the words, I noticed my heart was beating in my ears. "I really thought something had happened to you."

She was quiet for a moment. "Well, to be honest with you, I did doze off for a moment." She looked at me, pride spreading across her face. "I sleep with my eyes open. Do you know anyone who can do that?"

Before I could answer, she was telling me about her friend Delores who "claimed" she could sleep with her eyes open but, as it turned out, just slept with one eye half-open because she had a stroke and it wouldn't close all the way.

I sat there in silence before saying a quick prayer. My hands resumed their spot around the seat cushion and I could feel the blood draining from my knuckles yet again.

"So what was it you tried to talk to me about before you nearly killed us?"

I swallowed hard, trying to push away the irritation that fought to come out.

"I asked you what your name was." I stared at her and decided right then that I wouldn't take my eyes off of her for the rest of the trip. I would make sure she stayed awake, even if it meant talking to her the entire time.

"Oh yes! My name is Hattie Sue Miller," she said with a bit of arrogance. She glanced at me. "My father used to own most of this land." She motioned to either side of us. "Until he sold it and made a fortune." She gave me a look and dropped her voice to a whisper as she raised one eyebrow. "Of course we don't talk about money. That would be inappropriate." She said that last part like I had just asked her when she had last had sex. I felt ashamed until I realized I had never asked her about her money; I had simply asked her name. This woman was a nut. Didn't Grandma Dean have any other friends she could've sent to get me?

For the next hour or so, I asked her all kinds of questions to keep her awake—none of them about money or anything I thought might lead to money. If what she told me was true, she had a very interesting upbringing. She claimed to be related to Julia Tuttle, the woman who founded Miami. Her stories of how she got a railroad company to agree to build tracks there were fascinating. It wasn't until she told me she was also related to Michael Jackson that I started to question how true her stories were.

"We're almost there! Geraldine will be so happy to see you. You're all she's talked about the last two weeks." She pulled into a street lined with palm trees. "You're going to love it here." She smiled as she drove. "I've lived here a long time. It's far enough away from the city that you don't have all that hullaballoo, but big enough that you can eat at a different restaurant every day for a month."

When we entered the downtown area, heavy gray smoke

hung in the air, and the road was blocked by a fire truck and two police cars.

"Oh no! I think there might have been a fire!" I leaned forward in my seat, trying to get a better look.

"Of course there was a fire!" Hattie huffed like I was an idiot. "That's why Geraldine sent me to get you!"

"What?! Is she okay?" I scanned the crowd and saw her immediately. She was easy to spot, even at our distance.

"Oh yes. She's fine. Her shop went up in flames as she was headed out the door. She got the call from a neighboring store owner and called me right away to go get you. Honestly, I barely had time to make you a sign." She acted like Grandma Dean had really put her in a bad position, leaving her only minutes to get my name on a piece of poster board.

Hattie pulled over and I jumped out; I'd come back for my luggage later. As I made my way toward the crowd, I was amazed at how little my Grandma Dean—or Grandma Dean-Dean, as I had called her since I was a little girl— had changed. Her bleach blonde hair was nearly white and cut in a cute bob that was level with her chin. She wore skintight light blue denim capris, which hugged her tiny frame. Her bright white t-shirt was the background for a long colorful necklace that appeared to be a string of beads. Thanks to a pair of bright red heels, she stood eye to eye with the fireman she was talking to.

I ran up to her and called out to her. "Grandma! Are you

okay?" She flashed me a look of disgust before she smiled weakly at the fireman and said something I couldn't make out.

She turned her back to him and grabbed me by the arm. "I told you to never call me that!" She softened her tone then looked me over. "You look exhausted! Was it the flight or riding with that crazy Hattie?" She didn't give me time to answer. "Joe, this is my daughter's daughter, Nikki."

Joe smiled. I wasn't sure if it was his perfectly white teeth that got my attention, his uniform or his sparkling blue eyes, but I was immediately speechless. I tried to say hello, but the words stuck in my throat.

"Nikki, this is Joe Dellucci. He was born in New Jersey but his parents came from Italy. Isn't that right, Joe?"

I was disappointed when Joe answered without a New Jersey accent. Grandma Dean continued to tell me about Joe's heritage, which reminded me of Hattie. Apparently once you got to a certain age, you automatically became interested in people's backgrounds.

He must have noticed the look of disappointment on my face. "My family moved here when I was ten. My accent only slips in when I'm tired." His face lit up with a smile, causing mine to do the same. "Or when I eat pizza." I had no idea what he meant by that, but it caused me to break out in nervous laughter. Grandma Dean's look of embarrassment finally snapped me out of it.

"Well, Miss Dean. If I hear anything else, I'll let you know.

In the meantime, call your insurance company. I'm sure they'll get you in touch with a good fire restoration service. If not, let me know. My brother's in the business."

He handed her a business card and I saw the name in red letters across the front: *Clean-up Guys*. Not a very catchy name. Then suddenly it hit me. A fireman with a brother who does fire restoration? Seemed a little fishy. Joe must have noticed my expression, because he chimed in. "Our house burned down when I was eight and Alex was twelve. I guess it had an impact on us."

Grandma Dean took the card and put it in her back pocket. "Thanks, Joe. I'll give Alex a call this afternoon."

They said their good-byes and as Joe walked away, Grandma Dean turned toward me. "What did I tell you about calling me 'Grandma' in public?" Her voice was barely over a whisper. "I've given you a list of names that are appropriate and I don't understand why you don't use one of them!"

"I'm not calling you Coco!" My mind tried to think of the other names on the list. Peaches? Was that on there? Whatever it was, they all sounded ridiculous.

"There is nothing wrong with Coco!" She pulled away from me and ran a hand through her hair as a woman approached us.

"Geraldine, I'm so sorry to hear about the fire!" The woman hugged Grandma Dean. "Do they know what started it?"

"No, but Joe's on it. He'll figure it out. I'm sure it was wiring or something. You know how these old buildings are."

The woman nodded in agreement. "If you need anything, please let me know." She hugged Grandma again and gave her a look of pity.

"Bev, this is my…daughter's daughter, Nikki."

I rolled my eyes. She couldn't even say granddaughter. I wondered if she would come up with some crazy name to replace that too.

"It's nice to meet you," Bev said without actually looking at me. She looked worried. Her drawn-on eyebrows were pinched together, creating a little bulge between them. "If you hear anything about what started it, please be sure to let me know."

Grandma turned to me as the woman walked away. "She owns the only other antique store on this block. I'm sure she's happy as a clam that her competition is out for a while," Grandma said, almost with a laugh.

I gasped. "Do you think she did it? Do you think she set fire to your shop?"

"Oh, honey, don't go jumping to conclusions like that. She would never hurt a fly." Grandma looked around. "Where's your luggage?"

I turned to point toward Hattie's car, but it was gone.

Grandma let out a loud laugh. "Hattie took off with your luggage? Well, then let's go get it."

THANKS FOR READING the sample of *Up in Smoke*. I really hope you liked it. You can read the rest at:

- **amazon.com/dp/B06XHKYRRX**

MAKE sure you turn to the next page for the preview of *A Pie to Die For*.

PREVIEW: A PIE TO DIE FOR

"*B*ut you don't understand, I use only the finest, organic ingredients." My voice was high-pitched as I pleaded my case to the policeman. Oh, this was just like an episode of Criminal Point. Hey, I wondered who the killer turned out to be. I shook my head. That's not important, Rachael, I scolded myself. *What's important is getting yourself off this murder charge.* Still, I hoped Pippa had recorded the ending of the episode.

I tried to steady my breathing as Jackson—Detective Whitaker—entered the room and threw a folder on the table, before studying the contents as though he was cramming for a test he had to take the next day. He rubbed his temples and frowned.

Is he even going to make eye contact with me? Is he just going to completely ignore the interaction we had at the fair? Pretend it never even happened.

"Jackson..." I started, before I was met with a steely glare. "Detective. Surely you can't think I had anything to do with this?"

Jackson looked up at me slowly. "Had you ever had any contact with Mrs. Batters before today?"

I shifted in my seat. "Yes," I had to admit. "I knew her a little from the store. She was always quite antagonistic towards me, but I'd never try to kill her!"

"Witnesses near the scene said that you two had an argument." He gave me that same steely glare. Where was the charming, flirty, sweet guy I'd meet earlier? He was now buried beneath a suit and a huge attitude.

"Well...it wasn't an argument...she was just...winding me up, like she always does."

Jackson shot me a sharp look. "So, she was annoying you? Was she making you angry?"

"Well... Well..." I tripped over my words. He was now making me nervous for an entirely different reason than he had earlier. Those butterflies were back, but now they felt like daggers.

Come on, Rach. Everyone knows that the first suspect in Criminal Point is not the one that actually did it.

But how many people had Jackson already interviewed? Maybe he was saving me for last. Gosh, maybe my cherry pie had actually killed the woman!

"Answer the question please, Miss Robinson."

"Not angry, no. I was just frustrated."

"Frustrated?" A smile curled at his lips before he pounced. "Frustrated with Mrs. Batters?"

"No! The situation. Come on—you were there!" I tried to appeal to his sympathies, but he remained a brick wall.

"It doesn't matter whether I was there or not. That is entirely besides the point." He said the words a little too forcefully.

I swallowed. "I couldn't get any customers to try my cakes, and Bakermatic was luring everyone away with their free samples." I stopped as my brows shot up involuntarily. "Jackson! Sorry, Detective. Mrs. Batters ate at Bakermatic as well!"

My words came out in a stream of breathless blabber as I raced to get them out. "Bakermatic must be to blame! They cut corners, they use cheap ingredients. Oh, and I know how much Mrs. Batters loved their food! She was always eating there. Believe me, she made that very clear to me."

Jackson sat back and folded his arms across his chest. "Don't try to solve this case for us."

I sealed my lips. *Looks like I might have to at this rate.*

"We are investigating every place Mrs. Batters ate today. You don't need to worry about that."

I leaned forward and banged my palm on the table. "But I do need to worry about it! This is my job, my livelihood... my life on the line. If people think I am to blame, that will be the final nail in my bakery's coffin!" Oh, what a day. And I'd thought it was bad enough that I hadn't gotten any customers at my stand. Now I was being accused of killing a woman!

I could have sworn I saw a flicker of sympathy finally crawl across Jackson's face. He stood up and readjusted his tie, but he still refused to make full eye contact. "You're free to go, Miss Robinson," he said gently. There was that tone from earlier, finally. He seemed recognizable as a human at long last.

"Really?"

He nodded. "For the moment. But we might have some more questions for you later, so don't leave town."

I tried to make eye contact with him as I left, squirreling out from underneath his arm as he held the door open for me, but he just kept staring at the floor.

Did that mean he wasn't coming back to my bakery after all?

~

PIPPA WAS STILL WAITING for me when I returned home later that evening. There was a chill in the air, which meant that I headed straight for a blanket and the fireplace when I finally crawled in through the door. Pippa shot me a sympathetic look as I curled up and crumbled in front of the flames. *How had today gone so wrong, so quickly?*

"I recorded the last part of the show," Pippa said softly. "If you're up for watching it."

I groaned and lay on the carpet, my back straight against the floor like I was a little kid. "I don't think I can stomach it after what I just went through. Can you believe it? Accusing ME of killing Mrs. Batters? When I *know* that Bakermatic is to blame. I mean, Pippa, they must be! But this detective wouldn't even listen to me when I was trying to explain Bakermatic's dodgy practices to him."

Pippa leaned forward and took the lid off a pot, the smell of the brew hitting my nose. "Pippa, what is that?"

She grinned and stirred it, which only made the smell worse. I leaned back and covered my nose. "Thought it might be a bit heavy for you. I basically took every herb, tea, and spice that you had in your cabinet and came up with this! I call it 'Pippa's Delight'!"

"Yeah well, it doesn't sound too delightful." I sat up and scrunched up my nose. "Oh, what the heck—pour me a cup."

"Are you sure?" Pippa asked with a cheeky grin.

"Go on. I'll be brave."

I braced myself as the brown liquid hit the white mug.

It was as disgusting as I had imagined, but at least it made me laugh when the pungent concoction hit my tongue. Pippa always had a way of cheering me up. If it wasn't her unusual concoctions, or her ever changing hair color— red this week but pink the last, and purple a week before that—then it was her never-ending array of careers and job changes that entertained me and kept me on my toes. When you're trying to run your own business, forced to be responsible day in and day out, you have to live vicariously through some of your more free-spirited friends. And Pippa was definitely that: free-spirited.

"Hey!" I said suddenly, as an idea began to brew in my brain. I didn't know if it was the tea that suddenly brought all my senses to life or what it was, but I found myself slamming my mug on the table with new found enthusiasm. "Pippa, have you got a job at the moment?" I could never keep up with Pippa's present state of employment.

She shrugged as she kicked her feet up and lay back on the sofa. "Not really! I mean, I've got a couple of things in the works. Why's that?"

I pondered for a moment. "Pippa, if you could get a job at Bakermatic, you could see first hand what they're up to!" My voice was a rush of excitement as I clapped my hands together. "You would get to find out the ways they cut corners, the bad ingredients they use, and, if you were really lucky, you might even overhear someone say something about Mrs. Batters!"

A gleam appeared in Pippa's green eyes. "Well, I do need a job, especially after today."

I raced on. "Yes! And you've got plenty of experience working in cafes."

"Yeah. I've worked in hundreds of places." She took a sip of the tea and managed to swallow it. She actually seemed to enjoy it.

"I know you've got a lot of experience. You're sure to get the job. They're always looking for part-timers." Unfortunately, Bakermatic was planning on expanding the storefront even further, and that meant they were looking for even more employees to fill their big yellow store. "Pippa, this is the perfect plan! We'll get you an application first thing in the morning. Then you can start investigating!"

Pippa raised her eyebrows. "Investigating?"

I nodded and lay my head back down on the carpet. "Criminal Point—Belldale Style! Bakery Investigation Unit! I will investigate and do what I can from my end as well! Perhaps I could talk to people from all the other food stalls! Oh, Pippa, we're going to make a crack team of detectives!"

"The Bakery Detectives!"

We both started giggling but, as the full weight of the day's events started to pile up on me, I felt my stomach tighten. It might seem fun to send Pippa in to spy on

Bakermatic, but this was serious. My bakery, my livelihood, and even my own freedom depended on it.

THANKS FOR READING a sample of my book, *A Pie to Die For*. I really hope you liked it. You can read the rest at:

amazon.com/dp/B01D6ZVT78

OR YOU CAN GET it for free by signing up for our newsletter.

FairfieldPublishing.com/cozy-newsletter/

amazon.com/dp/B01D6ZVT78